THE CHARCOAL BURNERS

THE CHARCOAL BURNERS

Susan Musgrave

McCLELLAND AND STEWART

The Canadian Publishers
McClelland and Stewart Limited
25 Hollinger Road, Toronto M4B 3G2

This is a work of fiction. Any resemblance to persons living or dead is purely coincidental.

Excerpt on page 57 is from "Stones, Bones and Skin: Ritual and Shamanic Art," *Artscanada*

CANADIAN CATALOGUING IN PUBLICATION DATA

Musgrave, Susan, 1951-
The charcoal burners

ISBN 0-7710-6650-3

I. Title.
PS8576.U8C52 C813'.54 C80-094482-8
PR9199.3.M84C52

Printed in the United States of America

To Mike and to Helen

ACKNOWLEDGEMENTS

"East Oyster" was first published, in an unrevised form, in *The Canadian Fiction Magazine.*

Selections from "Old Mystic" were published in *Aurora 1979* (Doubleday) and broadcast on the CBC's *Anthology.*

I would like to thank all of the following who gave comment, information and support: Daphne Trelawny, Illtyd Perkins, Ned Brown, Christopher Brown, George MacBeth, Sean Virgo, Port Clements Volunteer Fire Department, The Bounty Hunters Motorcycle Club, The Canada Council, Sidney H. Smith, Ron McNeil, Peter Gzowski, Liz Twelvetrees, Ronnie Drew, Jeffrey Green, Bayla Schecter, Jennifer Glossop, Matt Jones, Haywire Dick, Jimmy Hart, Peggy Green, the people of Kung, Claude Davidson, Celia Duthie, the Skidegate ladies, David Phillips, Lyvia Morgan Brown, Ai, Frank Robinson, Robert Enright, Margaret Ring, the Sussex Archives, Adrian Batterbury, Jamie Angus.

Part One
East Oyster

1

Every week Matty scanned the Obituaries which immediately followed Births and Marriages in the classified section of the *Onanuga Oracle.* Due to a relaxed atmosphere in the *Oracle*'s composing room the dead could often be found under Miscellaneous For Sale, or under Help Wanted. It never made any difference to her – inevitably the dead were people she didn't know. Still she anticipated the column with a curious foreboding, half expecting to find her own name prematurely listed among those paid-up subscribers recently deceased.

The Birth notices were depressing; everybody had babies. She scorned that column announcing offshoots of futile couplings, ignored the subsequent marriages.

The Out-of-Town Personals were more inspiring. "Billy come home you can have long hair" signed "Concerned Parents in San Diego." Two women wanting love with means. A swinging bachelor into out-of-town culture.

And one day, at last, a message for her: "Martha Seeweed. Call home. Your mother is gone. Regretfully, Dad." As if her mother had gone out shopping and never come back. Had her father lost his mind? A telegram would have been more appropriate, or even a discreet postcard. Aunt Dot could have telephoned if he hadn't had the nerve.

The whole town would be talking about it. Death was everybody's business in a small community, just as babies were by-products. But Matty did not want to share this death with anyone, not even Dan, who decided, out of spite, to attend the funeral. Dan was the last person her mother would have invited.

They left East Oyster shortly after daybreak. Dan insisted on driving although it always made him irritable.

The dirt road out of camp was wide enough only for one vehicle.

"What if we meet a logging truck?" asked Matty, as Dan cut a sharp corner.

"We'll meet head-on," he said, accelerating.

She'd met Dan on this same road, four summers ago. Dan was working as a chokerman for the East Oyster Pulp and Timber Company, and Matty, in third-year anthropology at the University of British Columbia, had taken a summer job as a flag-girl with the Ministry of Highways.

It had been a slow, hot afternoon. The dust raised by the grader and by the few trucks that passed had settled over Matty as it had settled on the trees, the salal, the parched blackberries, the rocks. Everything lay sleeping under a layer of dust. Matty yawned. She felt her face crack like the bottom of a dry pond.

She took off her hard-hat and shook her head. The hat made her sweat and her yellow hair was lank with dirt. She wished she'd worn sandals instead of work boots, cutoffs instead of jeans, but the day had started badly with low clouds in the west threatening rain.

The grader was working in the middle of the road. The drone of its engine drowned out all other sound, and Matty didn't see the car until it was almost on top of her. She made a grab for her traffic control paddle – it was the first time she'd had to use it all week as most of the locals slowed down automatically – and waved the red STOP at the oncoming vehicle.

The car was approaching at breakneck speed. Matty

frowned, anticipating more dust. The driver gave no indication of slowing down for anyone, and Matty cast a backward glance at the grader.

The grader operator lit a cigarette. His back was to the car; it was travelling straight for him. He took a long puff of the cigarette and laid it to rest in the ashtray.

She imagined the scene: the grader reduced to a skeleton, its steel ribs gleaming with white heat; two men emerging from the heat-twisted car (a Pinto, she thought), incredibly alive but with faces unrecognizable; and a great black cloud mushrooming up into the sky.

She didn't have time to imagine anything else. It all happened suddenly. She heard the squeal of brakes as the driver swerved to avoid the grader. She heard dirt and gravel forced out from under the car's tires like guts from a crushed animal. She felt the whole world spinning; she tasted her own blood.

The foreman bent over her. She was stunned. A rock had grazed her head and she'd bitten her tongue in the fall. The grader operator came running to help but recoiled instantly at the sight of blood. The foreman mopped her face with a rag. His mechanical hands guided her to her feet, and he wrapped her in his jacket. The grader operator, recovering, offered black coffee from his thermos and half a cheese sandwich.

"I'll be all right," said Matty. She was shivering and wanted to lie down again. "What happened?"

The Pinto had rolled into the ditch on the far side of the road. Both bodies had been thrown clear of the wreckage.

"Are they alive?" she asked.

"Not if they're lucky," the foreman said.

Matty had been asked to identify him in court. Dan spoke on his own behalf. He was tall and lean, his face broad with prominent cheekbones and a high, aquiline nose. His eyes, though congenitally small through centuries of constant exposure to the wind, rain, and sun were widely set apart and slightly Oriental looking. His drooping moustache and full, turned-down mouth gave him a haughty look, and his straight black hair, which he seldom brushed, was gathered at the back and tied into a knot for his appearance before the local magistrate. Dan had survived the accident without injury. He wore a headband of red cedar bark, a buckskin vest, faded jeans, and elkhide moccasins decorated with beads and porcupine quills.

Dan told the court his full name was Daniel Joseph Seeweed. He said he couldn't remember the accident, that he had a bad memory for details. Matty couldn't swear that he had been the driver, but the foreman testified and Dan was convicted.

Christian Hawker, the passenger, had also escaped uninjured. He was sitting across from Matty and she'd recognized him instantly. Christian had studied with her at university; they'd gone to the Island together to do field work on one of the reserves. While he had talked to some of the young people about conditions on the mainland ("Boy, you sure got a good time over there, you sure got a real lot of people"), Matty sat in Granny Hannah's kitchen watching her five young grandchildren feast on Indian rhubarb and oolichan grease. The children called Matty Christian's "Mom"; Granny said that Indians liked Christian better than other whitemen who came to the village with tape-recorders and cameras. "He's get drunk, fall down, loses his money, just like a Indian," she said. He could hunt and fish, he could dig clams and pick seaweed. "He's almost as smart as a Indian!"

Christian recognized Matty, too. When the court took its morning recess, he slipped onto the bench beside her and squeezed her hand. "That's my bad friend, the one I was always telling you about," he whispered, pointing at Dan.

Matty grinned. She remembered Christian's stories of growing up in the village of Old Mystic. His father was a missionary; Christian's first home was a derelict schoolbus with the words OLD MYSTIC PENTECOSTAL CHURCH painted on the side, and FUCK YOU scratched underneath. When his parents were lost in a plane crash, Christian went to stay with the Seeweeds; he lived with them until he finished his schooling. Dan, who'd hoped to do "grade ten at least," was expelled in grade six as a troublemaker.

"He hasn't changed," said Christian. The prosecutor said that Dan had served a sentence for repeated liquor violations when he was eighteen. He'd also been convicted of possession of stolen property (his sister's broken lawnmower, he maintained) and theft of a picnic table.

The judge fined Dan $600 and suspended his licence for three months. Matty caught his eye as they were leaving the courtroom, and Dan smiled back.

They met for a drink at the Pink Elephant Cabaret in Onanuga. Christian ordered a beer, and Matty a tomato juice. Dan asked the waitress to put forty bottles of wine on ice, and said now that he wasn't driving he was *really* going to have a good time. "Once I start to get this stuff in me I can't stop, and then I start feelin' pretty good. You know, like dancing around and that. Sometimes if I get too much in me, well then I start to go haywire."

Dan was a good dancer. His eyes never left her as he moved her across the floor. Matty could hear the pounding of bare feet, the incantations of song repeated over and over. She could see the smokefires when she looked into his eyes, could see the ghosts of his ancestors celebrating the stranding of a dead whale on the beach, chanting and dancing wildly around the bloated carcass and gorging on rotten blubber. When she looked at him she could imagine the mask, Wild Man of the Woods, the cape made of skin trimmed with ermine, and a cedar bark hat. There would be strings of elk teeth dangling from his neck, woodpecker scalps and feathers hanging from his waist. She could even ignore his dentures, glowing as they did under the black lights. Their bodies were united in the rhythm of the dance, in the spirits of the elements.

They didn't sit down until the music stopped.

"I'm no good for anything," said Dan, "like a seal out of water."

Christian finished his beer and left. Matty drove Dan home later.

"Porcupine," he said, before rolling over and falling asleep the next morning. "You keep me on the move all night like a porcupine."

"Sexual intercourse! Sexual intercourse! Sexual intercourse! Get out!" These were her mother's parting words when Matty announced she was leaving home to live with Dan.

"Sex is nothing to get excited about," said her father.

When she married Dan, a year later, her mother refused to come to the wedding. She would sooner die than have her daughter breed with an Indian.

"Face it," Dan said. "She died."

At the funeral it was raining. Matty stood next to her father, sharing his old umbrella.

"I hope she doesn't decide to wake up now," he said, as if death were psychosomatic. "She always suffered from claustrophobia, your mother. She hated elevators. If she did wake up now the shock would almost certainly finish her. It would be the kindest thing, I suppose. Better than suffocating inside her own coffin."

Matty gave her father a look meant to silence him, but he kept on talking.

"Edgar Allan Poe had the same fear. Mother used to read his stuff–not bad, a lot of it. He planned to have a bell installed on his grave with a little rope leading down into the coffin so he could alarm somebody if he happened to wake up. Evidently the rope broke as they were burying him and nobody bothered to repair it. People assume that once you're dead these matters are of relatively little importance."

Matty and the gravedigger exchanged glances. Would the rain ever let up? The gravedigger kept staring off into the clouds. Her father was embarrassing. And Dan–Dan was picking his teeth, in public, again.

The gravedigger missed nothing. He was probably intending to write a book about his experiences. Matty imagined he was an undercover sociologist–they did that sort of thing. "Graveside Manners of the Upwardly Mobile." The suit he was wearing made him look like one of the family.

Matty blushed. Why should she care what he was thinking anyway, even if he were a sociologist. What if he had noticed her steady hand, her irritation with the others, her sudden interest in *him.*

He wasn't bad looking, as far as gravediggers went. If Dan hadn't been around she would have asked him for a drink, lured him from the book he was writing. Afterwards they would climb out of their funereal clothes and lie down naked on a strange bed. With her luck he would be unable to get an erection. Men were obsolete, anyway, according to a magazine she'd read, because of the nature of the female orgasm.

Matty looked at her father again feeling sorrier than ever for him as he tried manfully to light his pipe with a sodden match. She saw the sociologist make a mental note.

They stood awkwardly as the grave was filled in, her father rambling on about foreign morgues where the dead are kept in waiting rooms in case they woke up. Aunt Dot, who had been weeping throughout, burst forward with a bundle of red roses as if she had arrived late for a Valentine's party. Her petticoat had slipped several inches below the hem of her black knee-length skirt, and her face was sandwiched like cake filling between black hat and raincoat.

Aunt Dot was whining about the rain spoiling the roses; Matty wanted to strangle her. Her father droned on and on and on. She felt like goring him with Dan's toothpick. Dan was worrying, she could tell, about the imminent hockey game.

She tried to focus; the rain was forcing its own tears down her face. She stood by herself looking up at the trees, trees that had been selected for their simple root systems. Blowzy and voluptuous, they looked out of place in a graveyard.

The grave was piled high and little pools of water were beginning to collect wherever the shovel had left an opportunity. It was horrible to imagine, her mother being down there. What if her father was right, what if she *did* decide to wake up after all?

A clod of dirt rolled down the side of the grave as if something below had shifted. Matty looked around for reassurance but the others had started back to the car. She stood alone, watching the water that trickled in tiny rivulets to the base of the mound forming a shallow moat, then knelt to build a muddy bridge connecting the grave-island to the mainland cemetery.

Aunt Dot was huddling against the War Memorial where some ghoul had scribbled REST IN PIECES. Her father thanked them for coming. Dan removed the toothpick long enough to say it was the least they could do under the circumstances. Her father looked lost. Matty, wet and hungry, refused his invitation for dinner.

2

After the funeral they drove north. At lunchtime on the second day they picnicked along the river beside the Tote-Em-Trailer Court at Grizzly's Clump. A crowd of locals had gathered around one of the picnic tables where a travelling salesman was demonstrating his new Super-Electric Scrim-Saw. A dozen Indians had paddled across from the Kwikatsquee Reserve, and he promised to carve them an authentic Indian totem.

"...let's say you spend a year carvin' somethin' eh? Those old tools wear out and fall apart type of deal. Well, you get the same result and faster if you have one of these"–he held the Scrim-Saw over his head–"*and* you make money! We all wanna be rich, eh. Buy a car, maybe a skidoo. Well, here's your big chance. Have we got a carver in the crowd? Someone who volunteers?"

No one had carved anything on the Kwikatsquee Reserve since beer parlours had opened up for Indians, the man next to Matty was saying, except old William Williams who whittled a bit, and only when he got drunk. The man caught Matty's look, tipped his cowboy hat and winked. His partner, a fat man with red eyes, was watching Dan who stood some distance away talking to an Indian woman. Dan always stood out in a crowd.

"You there," said the salesman, pointing at Dan, "you

look artistic! Give us a hand, will you? There's nothin' to it, works like a charm. Plug her in and she's off. Come on up. It's a deal. A bargain."

Dan scowled. Matty, who was not in the mood for excitement, fixed him with a steely glare. She pushed her way through the crowd to take a strategic position by his side.

"Crazy fuckin' whiteman," he said.

The salesman was sweating. He cleared his throat and began again.

"What'll it be? You name it. How's about a buffalo? That's a good one! A buffalo!" He looked hopefully at Dan and then shrugged. Dan's attitude made him uncomfortable; he took the saw in both hands and flicked the starting switch.

The noise broke the tension. A few of the women squealed and covered their ears. Matty toyed with the fringe on Dan's vest.

She reached for his hand and his large fist closed around her. Dan took life so personally.

She'd tried to leave him. Three times she'd tried. After the first he'd followed her all the way to Vancouver, broken down and cried and begged her to come back. The second time he'd threatened to kill himself, and the last time–she was packed and ready to leave when Dan came home unexpectedly–he'd shot all four tires off the car and broken her right arm.

Dan needed her. She had agreed, again, to a reconciliation.

The salesman paused to wipe his forehead. All eyes were upon him as he made his first cut. The blade ripped into the heart of the grain, deep down into the profound Spirit of Buffalo. Sawdust sprayed the crowd as a crumpled horn emerged from the cedar block. One horn, one eye, a mouth, and a beak. The Indians, who had never seen a real buffalo, were impressed.

The salesman switched off the saw. "There you have it," he said, standing back to admire his creation. "A one-of-a-kind original, if I do say so myself."

Suddenly, unexpectedly, Dan began to laugh. Heads turned; the salesman coughed. The Indians looked from one to the other.

The salesman stood perfectly still, like a stranger confronting a hostile dog, holding the saw in front of him. The Indians began to whisper, urging Dan on. The man in the cowboy hat made a menacing gesture towards him.

Dan dropped Matty's hand. He stopped laughing. She glanced up at him. His cheek was twitching – a bad sign – and his lips were pinched. She laid her hand on his arm, felt the muscle flex.

"Dan," she whispered, "leave him alone . . . please!"

Dan pushed her aside and strode towards the picnic table. He stood face to face with the travelling salesman.

The salesman extended his hand. "Howdy," he grinned. "Glad to see you've – "

"Your saw is a hunk of shit," said Dan.

"Hold on," said the salesman, his grin spreading like an infection, "now hold on a minute, sonny. We don't want trouble, eh, so don't get your shirt in a knot. Calm down. Relax. Be reasonable, okay? Now what can I do you for?" He laughed, heroically. His face showed signs of strain.

"Nobody laughs at *me*," said Dan, tight-fisted.

The salesman threw up his arms defensively. "Wait a minute. Who's laughing?" He backed away, looking beseechingly at the crowd, trying to plead his innocence. "What did I do? Did I say something wrong?"

Dan snickered. He nodded towards the river. "Why don't you get your facts straight, mister. They don't have electricity on that reserve. They don't have buffaloes, either."

The salesman stood wounded and silent. He looked at Dan with resentment.

"They don't have money to buy your fuckin' shit," Dan continued. "It's assholes like you who make trouble for Indian people."

The whites in the crowd began to murmur.

"Now look, buddy," said the salesman, his confidence returning, "I don't know who you are but–"

"Don't 'buddy' me," said Dan. "That's right, you don't know who I am. You don't know anything about Indian people."

"I'm not trying to start a race riot," said the salesman. "I'm just tryin' to make a living."

"Fuck off and leave us alone," said Dan, "or I'll break your fuckin' head."

"You dirty savage," hissed the fat man with the red eyes. "One move and you're dead."

Dan spun round to face him and the salesman crossed himself. The crowd was divided into two factions now: the Indians hooted and the locals jeered.

Matty fought her way to the front. Cowboy-Hat and Red-Eyes were looking for trouble, and Dan, in his present mood, could give them more than their share.

She tugged at his vest. "Dan," she said, "you've made your point."

Dan looked at Red-Eyes and spat. He looked at Matty.

Matty motioned him towards the car. "It's no good here, Dan. Let's go," her eyes said.

He understood. There was a moment when he hesitated, but he knew Matty was right. He threw his shoulders back, and spat again. Then he turned and followed her.

The salesman grinned. It was more of a nervous tic this time but it was the most he could manage. He patted the saw and put it in a box. His hands were shaking. He patted the saw again.

By dusk the next day they reached Onanuga. They syphoned half a tank of gas from a car parked on the outskirts of town and then drove on to the Food Giant. Dan said he would wait in the car while Matty picked up their dinner.

She frowned. "I don't like doing this," she said.

"You've done it enough before. Just be careful."

She was too tired to argue. "What do you want?"

"A big roast, lots of fat," Dan answered. "I'm real hungry."

The Food Giant was closing and the butcher had gone for the day. Matty approached the meat counter warily, glancing once over her shoulder to make sure no one was watching. Then, selecting a prime rib roast, she stuffed it under her sweater.

The Muzak stopped, suddenly, accusingly. Wheeling her cart into a narrow aisle she knocked into a display marked EVERYTHING-FOR-THE-BARBECUE. She pushed on, nervously. The meat was heavy, cold against her belly; she felt pregnant, sticky, weighed down by fat and fear.

She paid for a Coke and some peanuts.

"What took you?" Dan said, when she returned to the car. "What did you do, clean the place out?"

Matty produced the roast – she'd managed to hold it so the juices didn't leak – and Dan whistled. "You're almost as good as my brother Dickie. That guy can steal anything!"

"Where's your can opener?" asked Matty, reaching into the bag for her Coke.

"Thirsty, eh?" said Dan. "Let's stop at the bar. One drink, okay? That's it. I promise you. I won't go haywire."

Once an Indian gets that stuff in him he can't stop. Over the years Matty had learned what "going haywire" meant. When Dan got drunk and behaved violently, the fault was not in himself he said, but in the liquor.

They drove down Main Street, past the Volunteer Fire Department, past the Public Health Clinic. Matty thought of all the times she'd had to bring Dan to that clinic to have old stitches removed and new ones put in. Agnes Burke was the clinic doctor, and Dan didn't trust lady doctors, but the only alternative was the Mission Hospital some fifty miles to the south. Dan was reminded of this fact every day as he drove to work in the beat-up company crummy. A large sign on the

Main Branch road read REMEMBER YOU ARE 72 MILES FROM THE NEAREST HOSPITAL. Sometimes that didn't matter.

"Remember that man? What's his name? The one you worked with when you were packing powder?" Matty asked as the waitress brought the beer. They were sitting by the window in the beer parlour at the Terminal Hotel. The hotel was opposite the clinic and Matty had a view of its neighbour, Custom Funerals.

"Yeah. Walter. What about him?" said Dan.

"I was just thinking," said Matty.

Dan's last job had been packing powder. All day he hauled fifty-pound boxes of dynamite from a storage shed and loaded them onto Walter's pickup. When the truck was full they drove out to the claim where the trees had been cut and the saleable timber graded. Walter's job was to blast the stumps. Dan hauled powder from the pickup into the slash.

"It's like an undertaker," said Walter, stopping beside a giant spruce stump. "You have a body–or what's left of it–and that's what you're going to get rid of."

Dan nodded. Walter dug a hole in the roots and loaded the hole with dynamite. "I reckon this butt measures eighteen feet across," he said. "You'd build a two-bedroom home out of the first log. You'd get a small hotel from the whole tree." He lit the fuse and motioned to Dan. They turned and walked away. Dan said there was nothing left afterwards but a crater and a bunch of chips.

He came home covered in sawdust. The second week on the job he started getting headaches–a result of inhaling the powder all day–and Matty, worried about his health, insisted that he complain to the personnel manager. Dan was promised a new job beginning the next week.

Friday was his last day with Walter. They went to work early; it was fire season and the logging operation shut down at noon. They loaded the first stump around six-thirty. Walter lit the fuse and, with the same match, lit a cigarette.

Dan, as usual, headed for cover. He'd been warned not to

run in case he tripped. When he'd gone a safe distance he turned to speak to Walter.

Walter wasn't there. Dan looked back and saw him sitting on the stump. He smiled to Dan, and waved.

The camp ambulance arrived after the dust had settled. Two ravens flew in circles around the clearing. Dan said they'd come for Walter's soul, they were undertakers.

Matty went with Dan to call on Walter's wife. She told them she didn't see much point in bothering with a funeral, particularly when there wasn't a body.

3

After five years at East Oyster with a clean safety record, Dan had been awarded a combination penknife-bottle-opener, his name engraved in orange on the back. He now rummaged through the glove compartment to find it. They'd left the hotel after one beer as Dan had promised but he'd bought himself a six-pack to drink on the way home.

Home was a small orange trailer in East Oyster's married section. The camp, headquarters of the East Oyster Pulp and Timber Company, was located at the dead end of a dirt road leading ten miles north of Onanuga to the Treaty River's mouth on the shores of Ocean Inlet. The sea lay beyond the mountains, accessible by boat, small plane, or four-wheel-drive over ungraded logging roads. Matty could hear the sea at night as it poured through the narrows emptying itself on the beaches up the inlet. She always went beachcombing after a storm. She'd found everything from a left-handed baseball mitt to Christ in plastic crucified on coloured seashells. She'd collected bottles from the Orient containing indecipherable messages, glass floats, fishing tackle, picnic baskets, shoes. She'd also found Albert's Harriet.

When Matty moved in with Dan, the trailer was a dump. The last occupants, a neighbour told Matty, had made an unsuitable marriage. Albert and Harriet never stopped arguing, and Harriet would take off in Albert's car. She always wore the same housecoat, hot pink, with her breasts hanging out. "You could see her leaving–all over town!" said Bette Millar.

Bette said they fought because of Albert. He was a real skin-flint and Harriet had no decent clothes. One night she took off and never came back. Bette said she didn't blame her: she'd leave too if it weren't for the kids.

Next day Albert stopped payment on the car. He moved out of the trailer and into the orange bunkhouse. "He's mostly an alcoholic now," said Bette.

Harriet washed up on a beach near the rivermouth; the crabs had eaten her head. Matty found her while she was picking salmonberries. Harriet was still wearing the pink housecoat.

Dan opened another beer. Matty was driving. As they left the paved road they met a herd of cattle. Dan rolled down his window, swearing at them, while Matty leaned on the horn.

"They won't move," she said. "What shall I do?"

"Go straight ahead," said Dan. "Run them off the road."

The cows were free to wander wherever they chose at any time of the day or night. They preferred the middle of the road and the middle of the night. There were often accidents which caused hard feelings between the loggers and the local ranchers.

Dan hit a cow one night, driving home drunk from Onanuga. The farmer had caught up with him and made him pay $500 for the useless carcass. Dan, wanting revenge, had taken to rustling the cattle.

Matty drove into the herd, pushing the cows aside with the fender of the car. Dan got out and prodded them on with his bottle opener.

"They're fat enough," he said. "Tomorrow I'll bring you hunting."

Matty knew the routine. They rose early the next day, just before dawn. Matty drove the get-away car while Dan rode shotgun, his rifle resting on the open window.

They found the cows browsing by the side of the road. Dan waited until it was almost light then chased the herd into the bush, separating the calves from their mothers.

His first shot was wide; he fired again at a yearling. She lagged behind, wounded, while Dan reloaded. He shot her through the shoulder and again through the neck.

The herd stampeded; the calf's mother stood on the road, bellowing. The calf fell to her knees, Dan gave her a push and she crumpled.

Matty parked the car and ducked into the trees. Dan was bending over the calf, his thick braids nearly brushing the ground. His body was glowing and he was breathing heavily, the way he breathed after making love. He always wanted her before they went hunting, wanted to roll her on the ground and make love like the animals.

The calf twitched and Matty jumped.

"Nerves," said Dan, "but watch out, she might kick."

The calf's eyes had gone dull. Her tongue was forced out at the corner of her mouth and there was blood, everywhere, soaking into the ground.

They dragged the body further into the trees. Dan took the calf's head in his left hand, twisting it upward. His right hand whipped the knife across her throat. Light flashed on the blade–Matty flinched–and blood gushed out. It was the knife that made her flinch, not the gurgle that rose from deep within the calf's body, nor the gaping wound at its neck. It was the clean stroke of the knife–she would live it over and over again in slow-motion.

The calf's mother was still bawling. Dan looked annoyed.

"She'll give us away if anyone drives past. Let's go. We'll come back later. It won't be so risky if we come back after dark."

Matty gathered dead branches and covered the calf's body while Dan washed his hands in the creek nearby. Then they circled round behind the mother, back to the road where the car was waiting.

That night they returned to retrieve the carcass. They carried it to the side of the road and, with great effort, hoisted it into the back of the Pinto.

The herd had vanished but the calf's mother hadn't budged.

"Forget about her," said Dan. "She can always have another next year."

Getting the calf into the trailer was more difficult. Dan backed the car up to the front door but they had a struggle to lift out the body. The wounds reopened when Dan dragged it up the steps. Matty followed with a cloth, wiping up the blood.

The steps would have to be washed, and the car. The coarse white hairs she'd seen sticking to the licence plate – she'd have to be careful to remove them.

Dan had the calf in the bathroom. They lifted it into the tub. Dan rolled it onto its back and slit open the belly. He reached inside the cavity and pulled out the liver. Matty took it into the kitchen where it would soak all night in a bowl of salted water until Dan ate it, raw, for breakfast the next morning.

Dan cut out the heart and the kidneys before drawing the entrails. He severed the head; Matty helped him with the skinning and butchering.

It was almost daybreak. They shovelled the guts into green plastic garbage bags along with the bones and the hide. Matty put the head in a sack. Then they drove out to the end of the wharf.

Dan emptied the guts into the water. They began to sink, slowly, but not before the first gulls of the day had sounded the alarm. Matty hauled the sack to the edge of the wharf and Dan pushed it over. "Crabs will eat everything," he said.

The seagulls shrieked and dived as the head sank from sight. The hide was floundering, water-logged. Too heavy for the gulls to salvage, it would drift and fall apart on the outgoing tide.

Dan cast a furtive glance towards camp, then headed for the car. Matty picked up the garbage bags and followed.

"My mother wanted to be a seagull–in her next life," she said, dodging as one swooped over her head.

"I bet that's her," said Dan, pointing out to sea. "Look what she's got."

An old grey gull, torn and battle weary, flapped along the water carrying the remains of the calf's neck. Matty had discarded it because a bullet had ruined the meat.

The gull was being mobbed by her relatives but the neck was too thick for her to swallow.

"She'll die before she lets go of it," said Dan. "Let's get out of here. I need some sleep."

Matty dreamed about the calf's head surfacing. She was swimming out towards it but the current kept pulling her back. Her sister was swimming towards it, too. Her mother stood on the shore waving a white handkerchief.

Someone was whispering her name. It was her sister's voice, a voice out of the long-time-ago darkness.

Her sister had drowned when Matty was four.

"Have you seen Jessie?" her mother asked.

"Jessie was bad," Matty said to her mother. "Jessie was crying."

Her mother had shared a cabin on an ocean liner with another woman. The woman had two children, one of them a baby who wouldn't stop crying. She said: "If that child doesn't stop screaming, I'll throw it out the porthole." Her mother went to dinner with the woman, leaving the eldest daughter in charge.

When they returned the baby was gone. "Baby was naughty," said the daughter. "Baby cried."

Matty hadn't pushed Jessie. It was an accident. They were pretending to be birds; Jessie played the young bird learning to fly. She wanted to fly over the well. Young birds must be brave, Jessie said. Matty, the mother, took the cover off the well. But Jessie couldn't fly.

Jessie fell. When she fell she screamed and the sound hurt Matty's ears. Matty covered the hole and flew back to her nest: when Jessie cried like that it was Matty who got the blame.

In her dream the calf was winking at her. Jessie was plucking out the eyes of her favourite doll. "Dolls don't see anything. Dolls can't feel anything," she said. Then Jessie cried because the eyes were lost.

When Dan cut off the calf's head Matty had touched the tongue. It felt cold and rough. In her dream she lost sight of the head but it came up underneath her and she felt the roughness again, this time on the sole of her foot. The tongue licked her foot until there was nothing left. Matty couldn't swim. The current was dragging her down.

When Jessie drowned Matty sat in her nest. She played by herself, pretending to be dead. Dead things couldn't see anything. Dead things couldn't feel anything. And then she cried because her sister was lost.

In her dream Jessie was surfacing. Matty was swimming towards her. The current was carrying Matty away. Her mother stood on the shore waving a tear-stained handkerchief.

4

There was a knock on the door. Matty woke, stumbled out of bed and pulled on her Stanfields. Whoever it was had gone. A pamphlet depicting a man whose belief in Christ led him to success in the doughnut business was lying on her doorstep.

She crumpled the pamphlet and threw it into the garbage. The clock hadn't worked properly since Dan had used it as a target in a knife-throwing exercise but she guessed he'd been gone for a couple of hours. She'd cooked his breakfast and returned to bed. Most days she slept until noon, her dream-life more active than daily life in East Oyster.

Yawning she opened the freezer and rummaged around for the deer's heart she'd seen frozen to a chicken breast. She'd have to use a knife to separate them now. Dan had been careless when he'd reorganized for the calf.

But when she found the heart it felt warm. She could almost feel it melting. The chicken breast was soft, too. Blood oozed out when she poked the calf's kidneys.

She imagined her hands coaxing life into the butchered remains. She saw her billy-goat grazing along the shag carpet, her pet rooster perched on the swag lamp, crowing. She saw her piglets, Bacon and Ham, mucking through the garbage, and Sexton, the bull, pacing about in the hall.

She stared at all the neat packages containing partially

frozen pets. She felt responsible for their various deaths. Whenever she got angry or criticized Dan for drinking, he drove straight out to the Old Farm – the company rented it to them so Matty could keep animals – and vented his frustration. So far he'd always butchered the males of the species.

Matty plugged in the kettle. The power was off; the men were working on the lines again.

The cold grey morning pressed around her. She gazed out the window into the grey marshalling yard, the monotony occasionally broken by the nod of an orange hardhat. Beyond camp it was the same – the scarred hills, the slash, the barren rocks, cloud, mist and mud – everything was colourless. The forest stood drab and pulseless.

She turned from the window. On the table the deer's heart had thawed in a puddle.

"Yoo-hoo! Anybody home?" Matty heard the screen door slam in the back of the trailer. "Bud got a fish for you. I'll stick it in the freezer."

It was Bud's wife, Angie Ward. Matty scowled. She wasn't in the mood for visitors, especially nosy ones like Angie.

"I'm in here, in the kitchen. The freezer isn't working. Electricity's off."

Angie, her bleached hair in curlers, stuck her head in the door. She saw the heart and sniffed.

"Ugh! Heart *again*, eh? Just kidding, doll. So what have you been up to?"

"Nothing much," said Matty. "You know, the usual."

"I know. I know *exactly.* Life goes on, eh? And your mother – I read it in the papers. It must have *killed* you. I hope she didn't suffer?"

"She committed suicide," said Matty.

"Bette told me. You *poor* baby. And the funeral, was it nice? Your *poor* father."

Matty took a knife and began chopping the heart into bite-size pieces.

"It was simple," she said, "nothing fancy." Angie, with her talent for trivializing everything, did not need to know the details.

"Anyway," Matty continued, "it's all over. What's been happening with you and Bud?"

"You know. The usual. Frontier living–the whole bit. Bud's bitchin' at me to go hunting next weekend. As if I got nothing better to do."

The Wards lived in Onanuga. At thirty-eight Bud had his first heart attack, at forty he developed an ulcer. His doctor in Vancouver advised him to retire early. Bud stepped down as vice-president of East Oyster Pulp and Timber, gave up three-piece suits for Levi's, gave up women for Angie, and moved north as the company's logging superintendent.

Frontier living appealed to Bud in his centrally heated house with all its modern conveniences. He bought a jeep that could go anywhere on land and a boat that could go most places on water. He traded the Eldorado for a GMC pickup. Angie installed a gunrack to complete his image.

Angie taught him how to shoot. She was an expert marksman and regularly won prizes in local competitions. Bud was proud of the fact that she could "shoot the pants off any man." Matty suspected she would shoot off a lot more than that, given the opportunity.

"So we're going hunting," said Angie, resignedly. "Bud likes a good time on the weekend, know what I mean?"

Matty nodded. A "good time" meant going haywire.

"When Bud's loaded he can't tell one end of a gun from the other," said Angie. Dan called him "Tsee-Pie"–the blunderer.

Dan was the first Indian Bud had encountered. Dan had "saved Bud's scalp" once when they'd both been poaching salmon. They'd stood on opposite banks of the river, ignoring one another until the gamewarden's spotlight made contact unavoidable. Dan knew the river well–there was no place to hide on the opposite bank. He dropped his net and whistled to his opponent. Bud, splashing across the river, made more racket than ten cougars chasing a pregnant bitch through salal, Dan said. They hid in a root-cave until the gamewarden stopped his search, and Bud said he was indebted to Dan for life.

"I wish he'd stick to fishing," Angie said. "You can't get brain damage from a fishing rod." She offered to bring Matty some deer meat. It was the best time to go hunting, she said, before the bucks started rutting.

"I guess we'll go one of these days," said Matty. "Thanks anyway but–"

"Listen, doll," said Angie. "Why don't we make a party of it? You know, take along some beers for the boys, a bunch of sandwiches. It'd be good for you to get out, after all you've been through lately. Give yourself a break. What do you say?"

"I don't really . . ."

"Sure, why not? It'll do you the world of good. The season opens Saturday. We'll get away early. Leave it to me, okay? I'll fix everything."

When Angie finally left, Matty put Bud's fish in the freezer. The power had come on and life in the freezer was returning to normal.

A thick mist had rolled in off the water. It settled over the roofs of the bunkhouses. By the cookshack Matty saw the crow; it had lived on scraps until the day it had grown bold enough to steal a whole sandwich from a chokerman's lunchbucket, and the loggers had painted it orange. They'd twisted its beak so it couldn't eat and broken its wings, though no one had guts enough to kill it.

The crews were coming in from the bush and heading for the office to collect their paycheques. Dan would be celebrating all weekend. After dinner he'd go to town and she wouldn't see him again until Sunday.

A truck pulled out of the marshalling yard with a load of cedar for the log-dump up the river. Matty watched it pass, its fog lamps burning.

Angie organized the hunting party. Matty agreed to go along–anything to keep Dan out of the beer parlour. He'd spent his entire paycheque having a good time the previous weekend. He'd vandalized a public telephone and terrorized the Boy Scout leader who'd taken his troop to the river for a swim. The *Oracle* spoke of "unspeakable atrocities." Dan was facing another charge.

"You should get a lawyer," said Matty. "You'll probably go to jail this time."

They were driving into the mountains early Saturday morning. Dan had been partying all night in the bunkhouse. He'd decided to sober up with a couple of beers.

"Don't bug me," he said. "I told you–I didn't do it. Blame it on the Indians. You're just as bad as the rest."

Dan had a point. The Indians were blamed for most of the crime in Onanuga. When Curlie Bob was found dead in a ditch, the coroner's report said he'd been shot by an Indian. When anything was stolen, wrecked, burned, or violated, it was always the fault of some "drunken Piute."

The road climbed steeply into the mountains. Matty felt like part of a military convoy. They had enough guns among them to wipe out the entire animal population. Bud was leading in the pickup while Angie followed. RIFLE SHOOTERS MAKE BETTER LOVERS, said the bumper sticker on the back of the jeep. Dan and Matty trailed in the battered Pinto.

"Slow down," said Dan, tossing his third empty out the window. "I'm eating dust."

Matty slowed down and Bud disappeared from sight. Angie pulled off onto a side road and Matty followed. They drew up behind Bud who had parked beside a creek.

They set up camp. Bud had converted the truck into a

camper where he and Angie would sleep, but Dan was going to build a lean-to, Indian-style. Matty did most of the work, cutting the poles and gathering cedar boughs.

Angie unpacked the picnic basket. "I've spent the last twenty-four hours getting ready for a twenty-four hour camping trip, would you believe it? There's enough food to feed an army. You boys hungry yet? You want to eat before you go out and play?"

Bud and Dan were talking hunting and fishing. Dan had finished off the beer and was starting on a bottle of Red Devil. Angie disappeared into the camper looking for her diet pills, and Matty went with a bucket to fetch water.

The huckleberries were still ripe. She picked them as she walked, finding fresh deer tracks everywhere. Most of the land had been logged off years ago, and some of it had been replanted. The deer came down to nibble the tender young spruce shoots, and this gave the loggers a good excuse to go hunting.

Where the slash ended, virgin forest began. Matty found a small creek and followed it upstream along a deer path until the trail became impassable. Here the trees were ancient, fungoid, overgrown with moss; often they had human faces. Their roots pushed awkwardly through the earth to snare a passing foot, spilled down again over the creekbank where they became sleek and silken at the water's edge.

The creek widened, fringed with devil's club and alder. Every ten or twenty feet along the bank were well-beaten deer trails leading out from the woods on both sides. Matty could hear a waterfall higher up on the slope. When she closed her eyes it was all she could hear, like the faraway sea in a shell pressed to the ear.

Her breathing became like water, heavy and secret. She lay on her back staring hard into the tops of the trees. She felt a permanent part of the creekbank, like one of the old cedars. She felt she could take hold and grow, send down roots, push upward towards the sky.

She was glad to have escaped from the others though they were bound to come looking for her if she stayed away much longer. Dan always worried that she would lose herself in the woods. "Just like a spirit," he said, "you make yourself invisible."

She took a deep breath; her skin smelled like the forest. Moss, decaying earth, freshly peeled cedar bark–even Dan with his keen sense of smell would never be able to find her.

There was no wind, no noise except the murmur of the creek and the distant roar of the waterfall. It began to grow darker. The conditions were favourable for a bear, Matty thought, the legendary bear who came sniffing around after women. He carried them off to his lair in the woods and there they had babies, half-bear and half-human.

Dan said it happened every autumn. When the salmon came up the creeks and the meadow grass was white with frost, when the ground had become soft mud and the women went digging for skunk cabbage, then Bear would come down from the mountains, looking for a mate.

Matty shifted onto her side, straining her eyes and ears. The forest was so dense it would not be possible to see the bear before he emerged from the brush at the edge of the bank.

She stood up, picking moss from her hair. Remembering her mission–she'd come to get water–she kneeled on the creekbank. The water was icy. She leaned over the bank's edge to drink. As her lips touched the surface she heard the shot.

She froze. The shot came from close by. A great thrashing about in the bush was quickly succeeded by a second blast. She jumped to her feet. A third shot rang out and she started in its direction.

It came from the other side of the creek. She crossed on a large water-soaked spruce log. The woods were quiet again except for the chirping of one small bird. A shrill gossip among birds, it flitted from tree to tree, leading Matty deeper into the woods.

A spike buck jumped up a short distance ahead of her. Matty suppressed a cry, but her sudden defensive movement startled him and with a leap backward he disappeared. Matty stepped through the moss as noiselessly as possible – she was scarcely breathing – pausing every few feet to look about her and listen.

The trail led like an artery into the heart of the forest. There was blood on the salal. Further along she found entrails and some stomach contents.

The path led to a clearing; Matty stopped when she heard voices. It seemed to her later that she'd stopped breathing altogether. The silence enveloped her, gave her protection.

The men stood in the open, the grass around their feet bloodied and trampled. Bud had his back towards her. She hardly recognized Dan who straddled the doe's carcass, spreading her hind legs apart. She was lying on her back, her head twisted to one side exposing the one eyeball that bulged grotesquely.

Dan was laughing at the awkwardness of Bud's position. Bud had his trousers down to his knees. Matty watched his buttocks rotating and heard him groan. He kneeled to thrust deeper into the doe's warm body.

Matty stepped backwards. The bird had gone, vanished into the shadows. Matty wanted to disappear, too; she wished she knew the trick of making herself invisible.

She heard Bud grunting and the *thwap-thwap-thwap* of his flabby thighs. He looked like a white rabbit humping himself to death, and his rear-end made an irresistible target.

Matty cocked her imaginary rifle. She fired, and Bud fell. Bleating he crawled for cover, dragging his one good leg. Matty fired again and the bullet struck his head.

Bud was finished. He stood up, slowly, and fastened his pants. Then he changed places with Dan who took the doe's legs in his own hands and pinned her to the ground with his weight.

This time Matty saw herself, wrenched and defenceless. The forest had closed around her. The only escape was in front of her, through the clearing. Dan's body rose and fell in rhythm with her heartbeat. When he breathed his breath passed over her lips and down into the pit of her stomach.

Everything was vanishing into a point of darkness. Her body was going to betray her again; she felt her tongue forced out at the corner of her mouth. Afterwards she couldn't recall anything, only a vague feeling of being swept away by a great river, and all about, strewing the surface in every direction, falling trees and standing splintered trunks.

Dan gutted the doe. Her stomach contained huckleberries and a variety of leaves; her udder was full of milk. After cleaning her and cutting some strips of skin for thongs, he dressed the fawn who'd fallen in her tracks and placed him inside the cavity, lashing the opening together.

Bud took a pot shot at a raven who'd come for the entrails, as Dan started up the path with the deer over his shoulders.

"Hey, Dan! How's she doing in there?" Bud called from the security of his bug-proof camper. Angie was inside listening to the weather report. "Hey, Dan! What's the matter? Don't talk so loud, I can't hear you!"

"Go to sleep," said Dan. "Go to sleep. I'm tired."

"What's the matter? Flies keeping you awake? I offered to trade places with you, didn't I, eh, Angie? Angie won't talk to me. Hey, Angie. What's the weather?"

Dan sighed. Matty lay stiffly beside him, staring up at the sky.

"Hey, Dan! I gotta good one. You see that movie *Deep Throat*?"

"No," said Dan, yawning. "I read the book."

"To hell with that! Pardon my French, ladies. What about the movie? You never got to see it?"

"It didn't get to camp yet. Remember?"

Matty heard the clinking of bottles. Bud tripped and cursed.

"Son of a bitch. You're ruining my joke. You're supposed to say, 'Yeah, I saw that movie.'"

"Yeah, I seen that movie."

"I bet you Richard Nixon had to see it six times to get it down Pat!"

There was a moment of silence before Bud laughed. Matty began to count the stars as they appeared one by one above her.

"Get it?" Bud roared, kicking over another bottle. "That's a pretty good one, eh?"

"You asshole. Go to sleep." Dan rolled over and put his arm around Matty as if he were afraid she would steal away during the night. Bud let fly with another one about not knowing what you were up against when a woman put on a false brassiere.

"Crazy fuckin' whiteman," Dan said.

The deer had been skinned and wrapped in cheesecloth. Their bodies were hanging in a tree, and when the wind got up in the middle of the night Matty was awakened by the sound of the doe's head thumping against the tin roof of the camper.

Part Two
Old Mystic

5

Grannie Gull was asleep beside a bucket of herring roe when the news came of her youngest son's death. Rose Littleblood woke her. Moses Seeweed's body had washed up on Halibut Rock. His boat had not been recovered nor had the bodies of Noah Jones and Major Bird.

Grannie Gull had not spoken for many years. She did not need to speak – the lines on her face told the story of her life. Matty called it "the face that launched a thousand herring boats." Grannie Gull-Glut.

She seldom moved from her chair; she had no need to move. Soon she was to celebrate her ninety-seventh birthday and everyone in the village honoured her. She sat in her chair, and slept, and waited.

At mealtimes she was carried to the head of the table. Her lips had sharpened with age into a beak, otherwise indistinguishable from the rest of her features. Occasionally Matty caught a glimpse of her tongue as she pecked at her food and swallowed without chewing. No liquid entered her mouth that hadn't passed between the narrow walls of a bone drinking-straw; it was bad luck for fishermen, she believed, if a woman's lips touched the rim of a drinking vessel.

Moses Seeweed had come from a long line of sea-hunters. Most of his life he'd been a commercial fisherman. His boat was the fifth to disappear since the herring season opened. The violent spring storms left few traces of the wrecks.

Some blamed the Book People who had come before Christmas, causing a spiritual unrest among the people of Old Mystic. The subsequent loss of the herring fleet was seen as God's retribution.

Those villagers who had remained sober enough to find their way into town spent long hours at the bar in Port Atchison story-telling with the Americans instead of staying home with their families and preparing for the Christmas festivities. Attendance at church was lower than it had been since conversion. To make matters worse, Spaghetti Chops came drunkenly to the Christmas Eve midnight service supported by Hogben on one side and Major Bird on the other. He was wearing a striped nightshirt and had a deerskin draped over his head. The skin was held in place by a crown of horns. Hogben and Major Bird were loosely clad in sheets. Hogben had a hubcap on his head and Major Bird a paper hat from a Christmas cracker.

"We three kings of Orien Tar," sang Hogben, winefully. Spaghetti Chops flapped his penis from a little hole in his shirt. Major Bird protested that *he* should be the Little Lord Jesus, that Spaghetti Chops was only an ass. Spaghetti Chops began to bray. Hogben stumbled over a corner of the sheet upsetting the potted poinsettia that had been flown in especially for the service. Spaghetti Chops tripped and fell on top of Hogben. Major Bird began singing a bawdy rendition of "Away in a Manger." The Reverend Thom Grady, who had himself been tippling, thundered from the pulpit, "Jesus Saviour pilot me! Won't somebody throw the buggers out!"

The congregation consisting of deaf, blind, arthritic old women remained, for the most part, unmoved. A few turned their heads and clucked disapprovingly.

Bad weather forced the journalists to outstay their welcome and a group of village militants sabotaged the camera crew's equipment. On New Year's Day the Mounties came from Port Atchison and arrested six suspects. The Book People flew out shortly afterwards.

Grannie Gull was sewing the button eyes on a stuffed frog; her fat hands bloated out from her wrists like drowned fish. The frog was a gift for a new great-grandchild. He was born on the same night that Moses Seeweed died.

"I guess Dan will be comin' home for the funeral," said Violet. "It sure will be good to see him again. He's going to bring his wife. I haven't seen them since they came here to get married."

She spoke slowly and carefully as if words caused pain. Grannie Gull rocked gently in her chair. She folded her lower lip down over her chin, acknowledging Violet.

"Dan's been workin' real hard," Violet continued. "He's got a good job logging. He didn't get laid off this year, not like last. He's just been workin', workin'. All the time he's workin'. He sures makes a good husband."

Grannie Gull nodded off, quietly snoring.

"Matty makes a good wife, too. She's got a real good education. I sure like his wife."

She tucked a blanket around Grannie's shoulders and removed the stuffed frog from her lap. Then she sat down to plan the funeral.

Violet's father had died in Vancouver. She had taken him there by plane, and there were doctors at the airport to meet them. Her father had been a dignified man. He had smiled for the nurses even as the claw inside him was tightening. Later in his hospital bed he asked for the curtains to be opened so he could see the lights of the city. Across the street a neon totem pole blinked on and off above an illuminated sign saying COFFEE STILL ONLY 10¢.

Her father had reached for her hand. She told him he would get strong again soon, that the doctors were giving him medicine. She would bring him back to the village where his great-grandchildren could visit. She would come every day to see him.

Her father had taken her hand and drawn it slowly to his lips.

"I'm sorry," he said. "I won't be there to welcome you."

Spaghetti Chops sat in a corner of Malaria Mary's talking to himself and minding his own business. He'd come into town to keep an appointment with a man from the Local Initiatives Program and he'd arrived early, just after seven, when Mary herself was the only other customer. Nursing a hangover, she was hunched over an eight-ounce New York steak and a bottle of Labatt's Blue.

"What the fuck do you want?" she'd growled as he'd shuffled across the room to sit at the table where he always sat. As usual he had to get his own coffee.

Spaghetti Chops had been unemployed all winter. Summers he worked in the fish camp on the reserve where his reputation as a cook had earned him his name.

"Spaghetti Chops" was a variation on a tired theme of Mary's. Spaghetti Chops had invented the recipe. *Half a dozen packages Kraft Dinner to one bottle barbeque sauce. Simmer until soft then mash. Form into chops and coat in batter. Deep-fry in grease until brown and hard.*

He scuffled through the kitchen into the bathroom. The door didn't lock on the inside and there was never any toilet paper when you needed it. A notice above the toilet read WE AIM TO PLEASE. YOU AIM TOO, PLEASE.

Spaghetti Chops had been an athlete once. Every day, as a reminder of past glories, he put on his shorts, his Green Flash running shoes, a limp T-shirt with U.S. DRINKING TEAM stencilled across the back, a baseball cap and sunglasses with vizors. Then he walked into town for breakfast. It was seven miles from the village to Port Atchison, and after breakfast he made the trip home again. By the time he reached Old Mystic he would be ready for lunch. Then he would turn around and begin the long journey back into town.

He became a familiar landmark for anyone taking the road between the village and Port. Everyone knew better than to offer him a ride. When he was younger he had run the seven miles and back. Some tourists had pulled over to offer him a seat but he told them no thanks, he was in a hurry.

Spaghetti Chops had strange dreams at night though he never bothered to tell anyone. He dreamed that the road he walked was leading him back to his mother's belly. He never arrived; after seven miles he was hungry again and had to stop for something to eat.

When Spaghetti Chops walked into town he had imaginary conversations with God. God, in his mind, wore a seersucker suit and looked like an official from the Local Initiatives Program. He would propose all sorts of projects, like making Old Mystic more attractive for tourists by using the designated dump rather than Dickie Seeweed's back yard.

Dickie himself had received one L.I.P. grant. He and three friends earned a hundred dollars a week collecting rubbish off the beaches. The object was to determine the origin of the garbage. Garbage was one of God's oversights and the Local Initiatives man returned frequently to Port Atchison.

"I'm not a rabbit either!" Spaghetti Chops was shouting across the room. Over a month ago Mary had served cold turkey for lunch accompanied by French fried potatoes garnished with a sprig of parsley. Spaghetti Chops had gone around telling everyone how he had left the French fries because they were too greasy and how he didn't eat the parsley because he wasn't a rabbit either.

Hogben sat in the opposite corner wondering if Mary had made the same mistake today. Secretly he wished she would lose weight and attract some new customers. He was tired of overhearing the same complaints.

Doctor Wynn Hazel was sitting by herself perusing the short list headed "Wine's." She was the newly appointed Public Health Officer in Port Atchison. Wearing a green tweed suit she sat with her ankles wrapped several times around each other and glared at the menu as if she resented the stale fumes and the lack of light. On the wall directly above her was a poster saying "If it moves fondle it." She hadn't noticed the poster so far but had focused her attention on the Australian calendar (last year's) that hung by the telephone and covered the flue.

"There's two flies stuck together back here" came a voice from the kitchen.

"Pour a bucket of cold water over them," said Mary, taping a Baggy onto the ceiling where the roof was leaking and the rain coming down near Doctor Hazel's head. "It'll evaporate up there, don't worry," she added, not wanting to discourage the new business.

Dickie Seeweed came in out of the storm.

"They found the old man's body," he announced. "I guess Dan and them will be coming back for the funeral."

He took off his boots and left them standing in a puddle by the door. "It sure has bummed out the old lady, anyways."

Hogben didn't say anything but nodded. Spaghetti Chops burped. Someone in the back flushed the toilet. Mary brought the doctor her Monster-Burger which she paid for and left without eating.

Dickie cut a wedge of day-old raisin pie.

"I read my horoscope. It didn't have nothing about dying in it," said Hogben.

6

"I'm not trying to kill anyone, I'm just trying to preserve the wood," Dan snapped. He had carved a set of bowls for Violet and was applying a final coat of paint. Matty thought they should have been left natural and argued that the fumes were going to poison her.

Dickie Seeweed had called to tell them about Moses. Dan had taken time off and they'd driven up the coast to Old Mystic for the funeral.

Matty was mixing angel-food cakes in an old chamber-pot. After the funeral, in obedience to Indian custom, Violet would provide a feast to the memory of the departed.

"First my mother, now your father," said Matty. "Things happen in threes–I wonder who will be next?"

"Someone will be, for sure," Dan said. "Everyone dies. Eh, Grannie?"

"Grannie's going strong," said Matty, glancing into the corner where the old woman sat solidly in her wicker chair. She had on a black dress that stopped halfway between her knees and the floor. Her legs were bare and she wore two mismatched shoes. Around her ankle was a tribute to her rank: a ring had been tattooed by stitching a fish-line through the skin and drawing after it a nettle fibre blackened with elderberry wood charcoal. Her face was smeared with a mixture of charred wood and oil to show that she was in mourning.

"She only lives for funerals," said Dan. "The only time I seen her smile is when someone gets buried."

Rose Littleblood looked at him and laughed. Her shiny black hair was tied back with a red ribbon; she sat in the middle of the floor making wreaths for the funeral. There was a constant demand for wreaths in the village, and Rose made the best arrangements. Every year she won prizes at the Annual Plastic Flower Exhibition in Port Atchison.

"Hogben was barred from church," said Rose. "Dickie told me. He left a safe on the collection plate when the Reverend gave a speech about being tempted and that. It was a *used* safe, too. Dorette says he washes them out and uses them over again. I sure felt sick when Dorette told me that!"

Rose stood up and stretched, rolling her lazy eyes at Dan. She hitched up her skirt even higher, and shook loose her hair.

"Since when has Dickie started going to church?" asked Dan. "I don't know why he still hangs around the village. He should move before he gets senile."

"Is he going out with anyone?" asked Matty.

"He's hustling some teacher," said Dan. "Blonde, big tits, been to school like you."

Matty frowned.

"And she only goes with Indians," Rose sniggered. "She gives it away–free!"

Matty knew Rose disliked her. Rose resented white girls mixing with Indians; she had been Dan's woman before he left the reserve.

"I thought Dickie was in love," said Matty. "Wasn't she local? A social worker? You know the one I mean."

"Oh, *that*," said Dan. "That was years ago. Dickie seen her with some Chinaman at the bowling alley. I guess he got heavy and slapped her around."

"Where *is* Dickie?" asked Matty.

"Down at the bakery," said Dan. "I'm going to meet him later."

Rose grinned. "Bring me there, too," she said. The bakery was a favourite meeting place, right next to the liquor store in downtown Port.

"I was just thinking," said Dan, "last time me and Dickie went partying there was a real dandy fight. Dickie got his teeth punched out. Shit, and I had to get stitches."

"It was June, three years ago," said Matty. "Dickie had no teeth at our wedding, remember? You passed out. It was raining. You got pneumonia. We found you in the morning. No one thought you'd live."

The marriage had been Dan's idea. He respected Matty too much, he said, to continue shacking up.

They'd spent the first part of their honeymoon playing cards in the Port Atchison Hospital. Matty stayed in the hotel across town and was serenaded at night by cat fights in the lane. When Dan recovered they went to the bowling alley for Chinese food and took in two of the Three Torrid Sex Features playing at the local theatre. Matty's father sent flowers. She found them, dead, a week later outside someone else's room.

Rose went into the kitchen to help Violet. Matty opened the window and turned down the heat. The walls had been painted recently but they needed another coat. Matty could still see the wallpaper, little clusters of yellow roses shaped like the skulls of babies.

A year after they were married, Matty had a tubal ligation. She decided to tell Dan she'd had her appendix removed. Dan had never discussed having a family but if she told him the truth about the operation he'd say she was trying to castrate him.

"You're thinking again," said Dan. "What's the matter?"

"I was thinking about kids," said Matty.

"Whose kids?"

"Nobody's. Just kids in general. You know. Babies."

"Oh yeah? Horny again, eh? I've got to go down to the bakery. I'll get busy with you later."

Their love-making had been strained ever since the deer incident. That was six months ago. Matty had never mentioned the deer but she couldn't hold Dan without thinking about it. Dan hadn't noticed the change though Matty refused to go hunting.

She went into the kitchen with a chamber-pot full of batter. Rose walked out, slamming the door behind her. Matty heard Dan start the truck; he stalled getting into reverse. She wondered what they were doing in the truck. Rose had a wild laugh.

Hogben was asleep in his armchair. Dorette and Doreen were engrossed in a late morning soap opera.

"Jeez, he's stoopid," said Doreen, applying a final layer of Jellyroll Red to her stubby fingernails. "All's he's got to do is say he's sorry and she'll take him back." She had started on her toes when the table beside her collapsed.

"Dorette! Watch Baby!"

Baby swallowed a butt that had fallen out of the ashtray. Dorette swatted him.

The soap opera was interrupted by a closeup of a distended belly. RELIEF was asking viewers for food parcels and cash donations.

"Uncle Moses is a lot luckier than the rest of us in this miserable old world," Dorette reflected. "All that famine and lack of food."

"What is this, the news or what?" asked Doreen irritably. "Is he gonna go back with her or what's he gonna do?"

Just then Matty turned on the electric eggbeater, causing a major disturbance on the screen. Baby began to choke. Doreen kicked Hogben who was adding to the confusion with his snores. He woke up cursing, upsetting the dregs of last night's Red Devil. Matty came into the room with a cloth.

Baby's face had turned the synthetic green of the carpet. Matty wiped them both and sat down to rock Baby on her knee.

Doreen had given "the best years of her life" to a French Canadian logger who had ditched her for a switchboard operator. Doreen ran up a large phone bill trying to track him down. When Baby was born he sent a ten-dollar cheque and a postcard from Niagara Falls saying "I forgot asking you please send my rain gear."

Hogben blew his nose into a piece of old newspaper.

"Jeez you're disgusting," Dorette said.

Hogben, a fisherman, had met the twins at a party on Moses Seeweed's boat. Doreen had been the more accommodating; Dorette had driven him from the dock with an ancestor's canoe paddle. Hogben had plans to sell the paddle to a museum but it was chopped up for kindling in the midst of the evening's celebrations.

The paint fumes had given Matty a headache; she put Baby down and went back into the kitchen.

"I always feel tired these days," Violet was complaining. "It must be my bum heart. Doctor was real good to me last winter. I had real bad pains at night. I was scared to go to sleep. I was scared I wouldn't wake up even. Doctor gave me these." She poured some bright yellow capsules onto the table. "They're real good for nerves. Doctor said so. Go ahead, take one. It won't hurt you. You been workin' real hard all morning. Go on, take them. Doctor says I can get some more."

Matty took the pills and stuffed them into her pocket. "I need an aspirin," she said.

"You need meat," said Violet. "Gee whiz, I start to get real faint if I don't have meat."

Violet had bought a large quantity of oolichan grease for the feast and its smell permeated the kitchen.

"Where is Dan with that truck?" asked Matty. "We've got to start taking this food down to the hall."

Spaghetti Chops stumbled in, clucking like a chicken.

"Jake's been chasin' chickens again," he mumbled, half to himself and half to the three-legged dog feigning sleep in a box by the stove. "I say, Jake the bugger's been chasin' chickens. Jake, you bugger!"

Moses had shot off one of Jake's legs to stop him running deer. Jake still waited for his master at the top of the wharf, sniffing the air, a worried frown creasing his forehead. He waited for the tide to rise, for the channel to become deep enough to allow the boat's access. When Moses didn't come and the tide fell again, Jake slunk home to his place beside the stove.

Moses had taken him fishing once, but Jake was more sensitive than most dogs. He could hear the fish scream, a sound too high-pitched for any human ear, as they were clubbed to death on the deck. Jake had gone berserk, flailing and howling until one of the deckhands had given *him* a taste of the gaff. Since retiring he'd slept, waited for Moses, and chased chickens.

"You's all goin' down to the hall later?" Spaghetti Chops said to the stove. "I say, you's all goin' down to the hall?"

"We're waiting for Dan to get back with the truck," Matty told him. "We need to take the food down and get everything set up for tonight. Amos needs the truck for the coffin, too."

"Dan an' them's all drunked up already. I seen 'em, pissin' on some guy's hat. Where's Hogben, that squaw-humper? I can't find my damn teeth."

"They're in your mouth," said Matty. "What hat are you talking about? Where's Dan? You've seen him?"

"Some damn guy, I seen 'em. Chickens and feathers all over the damn place."

A truck pulled into the driveway, stopping as it hit the cement supports on the garage.

"That'll be them now," said Matty.

Spaghetti Chops shrugged and walked into the closet.

"What are you doing in there and why aren't you dressed?" Violet sniffed, appearing from the bedroom with an armload of potato salad.

Spaghetti Chops muttered something about his teeth and backed out of the cupboard.

"You have to die before you get any attention around here," he grumbled.

"You can't come to church looking like that, alive *or* dead," Violet said to her brother. "What a thing to say! You should feel sorry. You're supposed to act . . . you got to be . . . Matty! Where's my blue tablets?"

Violet was on the verge of tears. Matty produced a jar of blue and white tablets from the medicine cabinet in the bathroom.

"You look fine," she said to Spaghetti Chops, as Violet disappeared into the bedroom. "She's just upset. Don't take off. You're to help with that coffin. How are things going up at the graveyard?"

She was starting to feel as if she were organizing the whole show on her own. Moses, at least, would have been grateful.

"Those damn Indians," Spaghetti Chops continued. "They're *still* diggin'. That Amos he's so dumb he can't tell his ass from a hole in the ground!"

Dan and Dickie lurched into the room, their arms around one another.

"Whas' to eat?" asked Dickie, barely focusing. Dan disentangled himself and collapsed on top of Jake.

"There's stew. On the stove," Matty said, angrily. "Where have you two been? We needed the truck."

"Fuck the truck," said Dickie.

Matty glared at Dan who had suddenly decided that Jake was the most beautiful dog in the world, and also the most intelligent. Dickie sniffed at the stew.

"Smells real good," he said, wrinkling his nose as if Jake had farted. "Smells like a fuckin' sh'laughterhoush, eh Dan-Boy."

"How do you propose to carry the coffin in your condition?" Matty snapped. She immediately wished she hadn't said anything.

"Hey, Danny Boy! Hear that? Your ol' lady jus' . . . jus' . . . propos' . . . to me. I thought you guys were happy. I'm sorry to hear that, real fuckin' sorry."

"Many brave sh'ouls lie ash'leep in the deep," chorused Dan, imitating Dickie's accent. Unlike his brother, Dan didn't lapse into the native slur even when he'd been drinking.

Matty stormed out of the kitchen. She heard Dickie opening a bottle of beer and Dan ho-hoing for a bottle of rum. She thought she heard Jake sigh.

Her cigarettes were in her coat hanging in the hall closet. She rummaged about for them; the cupboard looked like a collecting depot for the Salvation Army.

She slipped on a pair of boots and left by the back door. The next time she went anywhere for a funeral it would be her own.

7

Old Mystic was a small village, hemmed in on one side by a dense growth of salal and berry vines. There were three dozen houses, twenty-six occupied and ten vacant, all facing the protected harbour as they had done in the past. Apart from the two-room day school, the small Anglican Church, Ben's Superette and the dispensary from which the Indian Health Service attempted to provide first-aid supplies, vitamins, Lysol, cough medicine, and aspirin, the village consisted of only the frame houses plus an assortment of auxiliary buildings used for outhouses, smokehouses, and woodsheds.

The road, running parallel to the beach, was well gravelled as far as the Community Hall after which it diminished gradually. Matty followed a narrow trail to the far end of the village. The path stopped abruptly at the foot of an old totem pole. The Eagle had fallen from the top of the pole and the base, supported by props, was beginning to rot. When a pole started to lean, Violet had told her, illness resulted. In the old days the shaman would have journeyed into the sky. There he would have straightened the Pole of Life.

The fallen beams of a longhouse were slowly being absorbed by the moss and the undergrowth. This was the old village site and most of the buildings had collapsed. Remains of vast corner posts and sloping bargeboards could be found further back in the woods. The houses had been square, and built on a scale (forty to fifty feet in length) in keeping with the dense forest around them.

When a house was abandoned, the roof was the first to go. *In the Northwest Coast House*, Matty had read, *the roof was equated with the sky. The main supporting timbers symbolized sky supports. As in all sacred architecture, the construction of the building represents the creation of the universe itself. Destruction of the sacred structures signifies the destruction of the spiritual life of society. When the roof no longer exists, the sky also has fallen.*

The bank dropped steeply to a narrow beach below. Spaghetti Chops' hovel stood between the bank and the water's edge. A fish-shack mounted on pilings, it rose just above the high-water level. The shack swayed during the wind and Spaghetti Chops said it made him seasick.

Matty walked along the rocky shore. When she looked back she could see the wharf where the villagers tied their boats.

It was a relief to leave the village. She never felt comfortable there; the streets were oppressively silent. The old women peeked out behind dingy curtains as she passed; the cringing dogs and the foul-mouthed children avoided her. She felt their cold curiosity, their withdrawn measuring. No one spoke to her but everyone stared. Their remote brown eyes told her nothing.

In the old days it had been different. The village was more active when food-gathering was the greatest necessity. The women dug clams, pulled roots; they dried salmon and prepared cedar bark for weaving. The children picked seaweed while the men hunted and fished. The dogs, too, were useful, herding goats down the mountainsides where spears and arrows could reach them.

"Savages," Spaghetti Chops had said to her, "you just want us to be a bunch of damn savages. Diggin' clams and eatin' seaweed. I say, a bunch of dumb savages!"

He was right. Matty cared more about the ghosts. But even

the ghosts in Old Mystic had died: nobody believed in them. Matty sensed their sadness as she walked alone into the quiet places, into the moss-world of the woods where everything became shadow.

She reached the entrance of the harbour. On the north side a recent landslide had defaced the cliff leaving a pile of rubble as a narrow promontory. At one time the dead had been buried on the clifftop, also the site of an ancient battle. It was not uncommon to stumble over a skull or a dislocated vertebra – even a whole skeleton – as one journeyed up the bank. Matty pulled an armbone out of the dirt. She'd seen the village kids playing hockey with something similar, using a dead cat for a puck.

When the missionaries had arrived they'd relocated the graveyard. They renamed the point after one of their archdeacons but the place was still sacred in the minds of the villagers.

Dan had taken Matty to Point James at the end of their honeymoon. They found a cave and camped out of the rain, eating abalone and mussels and whatever they could find in the woods. Life was simple until Dan ran out of tobacco. After arguing all the way back to East Oyster, Matty herself took up smoking.

The cave was no longer visible, its entrance concealed under a ton of rock. Matty scrambled up the bank and found a good spot with a view of the village. She could see Dotty Lump-Mouth's clothesline, a notorious landmark. Dotty, who weighed nearly two hundred pounds, once had everything stolen from her clothesline *except* her underwear.

To the west was Halibut Rock where Moses was found, beyond that the open Pacific. It was low tide and a rich salt odour pervaded the air. Below her a starfish and a crab were stranded in a tidepool.

Matty sank back into the moss, closing her eyes. When she was a child she'd liked to curl up in the grass on a warm spring day, breathing the breath of the wild onions, the briar roses, the chocolate lilies. She would be quiet and invisible, talking secretly to the flowers. Sometimes she would fall asleep and wake to hear her mother calling.

She picked two pebbles from her pocket and placed one on each eye. Sunlight filtered through the clearing, warming her face. A flicker passed in wavy flight among the trees whose trunks and lower branches were covered with moss and ferns. Raven spoke once, startling her, but through his voice came the voice of a child, clearer and closer, a child's voice older than her own, drifting towards her out of sleep.

I am alone now. When I first came here I was lonely. It remains that the rest should be a part of the wind blowing all day long. Before I had been trailing across the field after my mother when the wind blew a flower into my hair. Its seeds exploded down the tracks of my face. I should have run then, quickly, to catch up with her– she was a long way off. But the clouds were gathering above me like the dark wings of a great dark bird, and the forests were stains on the ground below.

Shuffling my feet. Treading roughly over the damp earth. Wind and rain in my ears, the voices of strangers.

I lie in the grass losing sight of everything. I share a world with insects, a small sensation in an undetected place.

Then the sky is filled with the creaking of dead trees, the clanking of cold machinery. Steel claws are holding an open coffin. It swings over a cauldron of fire that everyone is watching.

I creep up, I am standing beside my mother. I have on a new dress with white socks to match and black patent shoes. The grass is long and wet and soaking the bottom of my hem. I want to start crying but mother has told me that I mustn't. You must try to laugh, she tells me, or at least smile as if you are enjoying yourself.

But I am being lowered into the fire. I want to sit up. Mother tells me everything will be peaceful. Rest now, she says, you will be sleepy later.

I look down at my body. I look up at myself. Hello, says the girl kneeling above me. You can open your eyes now. It will be all right.

Everyone is watching. Everyone is waiting. Hello, says the girl lying below me, sitting up and stretching. I see you've ruined your new socks.

Earth falling in on me, eyes growing used to the dark. Wind rising out of rain, washing me away.

There are wildflowers in the woods, there are owls who wake and guard the forest paths. Earth smoulders into ash. The rest is here.

Somewhere in her sleep she heard Raven and his friend-crows plotting to dispose of her body. She blinked and a stone rolled down her cheek. She had fallen asleep in the sun and the weight of the stones had blinded her.

She lay still and the blurred shapes of the totemic birds grew bolder. Puffing and cawing they came cannibal-dancing around her, full of their hideous appetites.

Her vision returning, she moved suddenly. The crows flapped off, crestfallen. Only Raven stayed behind to make quite sure, resting briefly on a mossy stump before flying into the highest trees to announce his disappointment to the world.

8

When Matty reached the village the funeral was in progress. There was no room left in the church so she stood outside the door peering over the heads of the pallbearers.

Reverend Grady conducted Moses's favourite hymn. Violet sat stiffly in the front row surrounded by sniffling grandchildren. Most of the women were weeping; the sound was almost song-like. Grannie Gull, who'd fallen into a fitful sleep, had been wheeled into a corner where she wouldn't disturb anyone.

A flashbulb went off as somebody took a photograph of the coffin, barely recognizable under Rose Littleblood's wreaths. Dr. Hazel looked alert. The first casualty of the day had already occurred when Spaghetti Chops caught his finger in the coffin.

Matty felt something rubbing against her ankles. It was Jake; Violet had forgotten to shut him in the kitchen. As the congregation began to leave the church she grabbed him by the ears and kept a firm grip until the coffin had been loaded into the back of Dickie's truck.

They had a mile to go before they reached the graveyard. Spaghetti Chops volunteered to drive since Amos Brown was missing. Dickie started the truck with a screwdriver and Hogben climbed in to navigate.

Matty walked behind holding Violet's arm. Dan, who had

sobered up since lunch, pushed Grannie in her wheelchair. The wheelchair was Grannie's throne; she sat erect and composed as if going to her own coronation.

The truck bumped over the road; Spaghetti Chops ignored the potholes. Hogben kept an eye on the coffin as it was tossed from one side of the pickup to the other. Matty was afraid it would fall off and injure somebody. Halfway down the hill they had a blow-out but Spaghetti Chops kept on driving.

"The only trouble with funerals is they make me want to die," sniffed Doreen, who'd run to catch up with them.

"Who would want to die in *that* old graveyard," Dorette responded. "It's too near the water, that's for darn sure."

The previous summer a government agent had come to Old Mystic trying to persuade the Band Council to move their graveyard up onto the hill. The agent said it was unsanitary for bathers: at high tide, he claimed, the graves were awash.

Jake whined pitifully, limping beside Matty.

"Gee, he's a real devoted dog," said Dorette. "I never seen such a smart dog with three legs before!"

But the moment they reached the graveyard there was more trouble. Jake threw a fit and wouldn't allow anyone near the coffin. Amos was found passed out at the bottom of the grave; it took three men and a ladder to raise him. Doreen led the mourners in a dirge while Spaghetti Chops locked himself in the pickup with a bottle of Hogben's parsnip wine.

Jake ran in circles, yelping, foaming at the mouth. He attacked Hogben, biting a hole in his wooden leg. A rumour of rabies began to spread.

Reverend Grady muttered a few words as the grave was filled in though nobody could hear him over the wind and the wailing. When Violet was saying a final prayer Jake broke loose again and began furiously digging.

"Jeez, he's crazy," blurted Doreen. "He thinks there's a bone buried there but it's only Uncle Moses!"

The women went back to Dotty Lump-Mouth's for tea. Dotty was a celebrity in the village, not only because of her clothesline but because an article had appeared about her in a well-known women's magazine. There was a photograph of her standing in front of her china cabinet wearing a ceremonial headdress decorated with ermine skins and the eagle crest (the large beak, the caption explained, was controlled by strings). Next to her stood the Queen Mother, also looking controlled.

The Queen Mother was touring. She'd been brought to Old Mystic to see the totem pole. She wasn't taken to see Dickie Seeweed's dump or the unsanitary graveyard. She didn't stay at the hotel in Port Atchison and the royal limousine made a detour to avoid Mary's.

Hogben, Dotty's nephew, had also had dealings with the Royal Family. He had been commissioned to carve a bust of Her Majesty the Queen and was flown down to Vancouver to make the presentation. The Queen was delighted and took Hogben aside to discuss native dancing. Hogben demonstrated his personal adaptation of Women-Conjugating-With-Spirit-of-Dead-Bear Dance and was instantly whisked away by the RCMP. Hogben told the reporters it was about time Her Majesty got to meet a real drunken Indian.

Matty sat in a corner of Dotty's living room feeling bored with the day. Doreen was discussing the colour of Baby's faeces with Mary Joseph. Mary had had an operation to stop her from getting pregnant; she looked pregnant again anyway and was telling Vina Adams how her tubes had come untied in the middle of sexual intercourse with two construction workers.

Esther Brown was describing her niece's marriage to a candy bar salesman – how they'd fought the first night and the niece flushed her diamond down the toilet. Dorette was reading aloud from the social column of the Port Atchison *Gazette.* Merle Eclair was the Best Loser of the Week having lost one pound two ounces. Mr. and Mrs. Darwin Rusk were returning from their second honeymoon in Disneyland. Marianne Alcott's Recipe of the Month was Pop-Ice-Pie consisting of two quarts unsalted popped corn, sixteen marshmallows (coloured or plain), four drops of almond flavouring, and a quart of vanilla ice cream in a toasted coconut crust.

Matty felt sick.

"You guys gonna stick around for a while?" Doreen asked on her way from the kitchen with a tray full of blueberry cupcakes. "Dickie an' them are goin' fishin'. Why doesn't Dan go? You could stay with us? Why don't you?"

"Thanks," said Matty, refusing another piece of Jewish shortbread (Esther explained it was made with margarine instead of butter). "Dan's got a good job. We've got to get back. Maybe we'll come here next winter. We might do some travelling. Uh, no thanks." She didn't feel up to a Dream Slice either.

"Jeez. Travelling. Where would you guys go? You sure must be rich to go travelling!"

Matty heard Rose Littleblood saying some men are attracted by a girl's mind. She heard Dotty shrieking, "More tea?" to Grannie who pretended not to hear anything. Anna Frank said her husband was a hopeless old drunk. Dorette said you see a lot more old drunks than old doctors.

"Where's the bathroom?" Matty asked. Doreen indicated with her tray, still arguing that Dan should quit his job and go fishing with Hogben and Dickie.

"It sure costs a lot to go travelling," she insisted. "You should stay here with us. It's cheaper."

"We'd camp," said Matty. "Maybe drive to California. I don't know. It depends if Dan gets laid off or not. It depends on the weather. I haven't seen my father . . . well, not since my mother. . . . he lives there now. In California."

Soon after her mother was buried her father decided to sell the house and join his sister in southern California where she'd fled to escape the cost of living. Matty didn't feel like discussing her family, especially in front of Doreen who was a notorious gossip.

Excusing herself she jostled her way across the room. She went into the bathroom and sat down on the floor. She heard Anna Frank say her husband had smashed the glass ornaments so she'd brained him with a lug wrench. Now he wanted her back.

And then there was Doreen again, banging on the door, wanting to know if she could come in and change Baby.

"I sure like these disposable diapers," she said. "They're real dandy at parties. Here, hold Baby. Why don't you guys sit with us at dinner. We can come back here later and watch T.V. What are you doing . . . jeez! Watch Baby!"

Baby puked into Matty's hair before she had time to reply.

"It smells real stink, jeez. He must have eaten something. Baby, what have you been eatin'? Jeez, look, it's all over your hair!"

"It's nothing," said Matty, cleaning herself off.

Doreen smacked Baby, and Matty followed her into the living room for a second round.

"Baby was real good at the funeral, anyway," Doreen was saying. "He didn't even cry!"

"He sure looks like his father," said Mary Joseph, viciously. "He's got the same blue eyes!"

Doreen looked hurt.

"You sure got a big mouth, Mary Joseph," said Dorette, sharply.

9

Matty sat at the main table between Doreen and Violet. Dan's place beside her was empty.

Rose Littleblood had decorated the tables. Large bouquets of artificial flowers last used at Anna Frank's wedding had been dusted and rearranged to fit the more solemn occasion. Bowls of fruit–red apples and green ones, oranges, and bananas–cigarettes and souvenir matchbooks were placed before each guest. Pitchers of Tang and lemonade, plates of sandwiches cut to resemble hearts but shaped more like miniature toilet seats, platters of chicken, turkey, ham, and beef, potato salads and jellied salads and dozens of angel-food cakes smothered with Dream-Whip adorned the tables along with traditional Indian foods: bannock, herring roe on seaweed, peppered sockeye, smoked blueback, sea eggs and oolichans, devil-fish, minced clams, and Violet's specialty–abalone chow mein.

The room was overflowing with people. There were more than a hundred invited guests and a few uninvited who would also be fed. Someone was squeezing into Dan's seat and Matty shifted her chair to avoid bumping elbows.

Reverend Grady asked for a moment's silence. The villagers prayed with him that God, having "snatched one from their midst," would look kindly upon His children and provide for them always as He had done in the past. While all heads were bowed, Spaghetti Chops sneaked a chicken breast for Jake who was lurking under the table.

After Dotty's tea Matty didn't feel like eating, but it was customary, out of respect for the dead, to sample each dish. This was the Feast for Hungry Souls, a meal that took place after every funeral in the village. The church had another name for it but the villagers knew the real reason for the gathering. When the food was eaten Moses could enter eternity on a full stomach.

Grannie Gull was lost in the mural on the back wall showing how Old Mystic had looked when she was young. A line of longhouses on a curved beach faced the sea; there were totem poles in front of the houses and a row of big canoes. An old woman was digging clams at the water's edge and an eagle the size of a pterodactyl was winging its way towards Halibut Rock. There was a Wurlitzer against the wall–it looked like part of the picture–and the remnants of a grand piano. The other walls were covered with prints that looked like premiums from savings stamp redemption centres–lofty birch trees in autumn, a sunset over the Rockies, a family of ducks being sighted by hunters. There was an outdated portrait of the Queen over the ladies' toilet. The men had to go outside.

Matty squirmed on her metal seat. Doreen was telling her how the lumberjack kicked her in the stomach when she told him Baby was coming. Mary Joseph said her five sisters married whitemen. Grannie Gull chanted an old song in her native tongue. Spaghetti Chops told her to sing "Snowbird."

Violet loaded Matty's plate with slices of roast beef.

"Gee, you're picky," Violet said, "Dan should fatten you up. You're too skinny. You're like Indian goose. Always pecking!"

To leave the meat would be an insult to Violet. Matty waited till she turned away before slipping it back on its platter.

She toyed with her salad, focusing on the hands next to hers. The long, sensitive fingers could have belonged to a woman, but the wrists were thick and the watchstrap definitely a man's. She recognized the ring–one of Amos Brown's creations. A wolf running in circles, biting his own tail, was swallowing himself in the process.

It was Christian. She leaned over the juice container to kiss him. His blue eyes were ringed with charcoal to protect them from the sun's glare out on the water.

"I wondered when you'd recognize me! I came as soon as I heard. We were fishing. They got us on the radio telephone. I'm sorry I missed the church service. I heard old Moses got a full house anyway."

"Standing room only," said Matty. "Poor Jake, he really went haywire."

"Pass the grease," said Doreen, trying to strike up her own conversation with Christian.

"She means oolichan grease," said Matty, as he reached for the butter. "You better watch out for her. She's been drinking all evening."

"So what else is new?" Christian laughed. "I get letters from Violet. She keeps me in touch. I heard when you got married. I was going to write to you back then, but I was having my own problems."

His wife, Eltheeda, had left him. After a seven-year marriage she'd gone back to the Blood Reserve taking their two sons with her. Christian had been teaching in the east since his last visit to Onanuga. He'd quit his job to come west and go fishing. He was planning to work a trapline in the winter.

Hogben proposed a toast. He stood up on his chair wearing the suit he'd bought to be buried in himself. He seemed uncomfortable because it didn't fit. He'd wrapped a piece of rope around his waist to hold up the trousers.

He cleared his throat. His black eyes squinted, assessing and evaluating the wall in front of him.

"He forgot his glasses," whispered Violet. "He can't see anything without those glasses."

Hogben produced a scrap of paper from his pocket. At the hairline on his high forehead tiny drops of sweat were beginning to form. There were some straggly whiskers sprouting on his chin; he was trying, unsuccessfully, to grow a moustache.

He unfolded his speech. He looked at it for a long time before folding it up again and stuffing it back in his pocket.

"He can't read a word without his glasses," Violet repeated. "I told him to bring them. I told him, 'Bring your glasses.'"

Hogben's voice was dry, grating. "The Reverend here – he said a lot of things at the church. The right words, prayers, you can call them that. Maybe there's not so much to say anymore. There used to be a lot of things to say, special things. We still say some of them."

"He doesn't know what to say," said Violet under her breath. "I can tell he forgets by the way he starts sweating."

Hogben looked at the Reverend. "When my great-grandfather was alive, well, there wasn't a church then. There was no minister, either. When he died it was in that Big House up there, the end of the village. The way we took him out was we took two boards – they were just laying around so we figured to use them before someone else got the idea, two-by-twelve boards – and we hauled him out that way."

Doreen started to moan. Hogben's brown cheeks deepened in colour.

"Well," he said, "that was in the old days. They sure could build houses in the old days, not like now. Anyway we buried him up there, the end of the village. My brother still stays there sometimes but my mother got some house she want me to live in so I moved back to where she is staying now."

Reverend Grady gave him a nudge.

"He's gone down the wrong track," said Violet. "He looks like a Chinaman when he talks like that."

Hogben cleared his throat again, concentrating on the wall.

He raised his glass in a toast and the other guests murmured approvingly. "So long, Moses. A good husband and a good father. Gone to the big logging camp in the sky."

Reverend Grady looked uncomfortable. Spaghetti Chops tugged at Hogben's sleeve.

"Uncle Moses wasn't a *logger*," protested Doreen, "he was a fisherman!"

Hogben scowled as he climbed off his chair. There was more applause, then the Reverend read a psalm:

"If I take the wings of the morning, and dwell in the uttermost parts of the sea; Even there shall Thy hand lead me, and Thy right hand shall hold me."

Doreen cut the cake. "You should go fishing. You make a real lot of money," she said to Moses's ten-year-old nephew who was sitting across the table.

"No way," he said, "I'm just gonna drink. I'm gonna sit around and do nothing. Get paid in a cheque."

"Jeez you're dumb," said Doreen.

Spaghetti Chops nodded at Christian, raising his glass.

"Merry Christmas, partner," he said. "I say, Merry Christmas!"

"He thinks it's Christmas," said Violet. "He sure gets mixed up when he starts to party."

Christian grinned. "I hear Christmas was a disaster," he said. "Spaghetti Chops told me about the Hangover Turkey."

Mary had been partying on Christmas Day and had forgotten to put the turkey in the oven. When Spaghetti Chops walked into Port for dinner, the bird wasn't cooked. He described it to everyone as the Hangover Turkey.

"I've never known him to eat anywhere *but* Mary's," said Christian. "I was surprised to see him here tonight."

"He's only come for the gifts," explained Matty. "He really cleaned up after the last funeral."

Spaghetti Chops was fumbling in the pocket of his jacket. "I should have spent my money in that beer parlour," he mumbled, as if he knew everyone was talking about him. "Darn that Mary."

"Every time he sleeps with her she rolls him," Matty whispered.

Christian winked at her.

"I never stole from no one and I'm not a hypocrite either," said Spaghetti Chops. "I don't know why that woman has to be like that. That's the way she is, I guess. I say, that's the way she is."

"What do you think if I marry the Queen?" asked Hogben. Spaghetti Chops stopped grumbling and looked at him in disgust.

Reverend Grady held up his hand for silence. It was time for the distribution of gifts. Matty excused herself from the table.

The women moved through the room handing out parcels. Money was given to the gravediggers and the pallbearers. Esther Brown made an announcement along with each gift of a twenty-dollar bill; Matty presented the Reverend with a carved cedar box. Other gifts included china, towels, blankets, aprons, linen, gallons of oolichan grease, bags of flour and sugar, cans of salmon and baskets of fruit. Violet gave Dotty a Lighted Pineapple Centrepiece for her table because Dotty had organized the ladies' tea.

"How's Dan?" asked Christian, when Matty finally sat down. The room was buzzing as people admired each other's gifts.

"It's a long time to sit for just one blanket," said Spaghetti Chops.

"Dan? He's still the same. He went to Port Atchison with Dickie and Rose. They were supposed to fetch Dorette but I guess they started partying."

"I was surprised to hear you'd married him," said Christian. "It's none of my business, but I thought there'd be trouble."

Doreen prodded Christian with her plastic fork. The oil

from the fish had left a little grease-slick around her mouth.

"You sure got beautiful eyes," she said, as Christian turned to face her. "Just like Baby's. You got real nice hair, too. Gee it's yellow."

Christian took the fork away from her.

"Where you guys goin' later?" Doreen asked.

"Crazy," said Christian. "Want to come?"

"I can't," said Doreen. "I got to watch Baby. I sure wish Baby would sleep all night. He always wakes up around four or four-thirty."

Christian poured another glass of Tang. Doreen began sliding out of her chair.

"Let her go," said Matty. "She'll feel more at home on the floor, anyway."

"Where were we?" said Christian. "I think we were talking about Dan. Why don't you walk back with me? They're going to start speech-making. I think I've had enough of this already."

Matty looked at Violet. "I can't go," she said. "Someone has to stay with her. You can have Dickie's room. The bed hasn't been slept in since we got here."

Jake hiccupped under the table.

"Can you take Jake as well?" asked Matty. "He has to be chained. He's grounded until the grave has settled. You, Jake you bugger! Come out here!"

Jake only responded if you called him by his full name, the way Moses had always done. Reverend Grady smiled nervously as the shabby old dog cast a disdainful look over his shoulder and limped towards the door after Christian.

10

Matty was having a baby. She had been wheeled into the operating room where she was given an injection to put her to sleep. Her body felt numb but her mind was still awake. They turned her on her stomach. Her mind registered everything.

The doctor came in with a fish knife and began filleting her back. He cut a clean wide strip of meat from either side of her spine. It wasn't painful because her body couldn't feel anything. There was no blood either, just endless white meat. By the time the doctor reached her shoulder blades, the nurses were hysterical.

"You weren't meant to have babies," one of them shrieked at her. "See, he can't find it. It's not in there. You weren't built to have babies!"

She couldn't talk, couldn't feel anything. She'd known all along there was nothing inside her.

She woke up reaching for Dan but Dan wasn't beside her. He had stayed out, again, all night.

She put on her dressing gown and went into the bathroom. Hogben's socks were soaking in the sink. He had rinsed a condom in the same water and it nudged the rim of the basin like a dead jellyfish.

She heard Violet cough. Violet had been up most of the night, drinking and eating tranquillizers.

Matty went into Dickie's room where Christian was still

sleeping. She sat on the end of his bed. He was dreaming, he looked peaceful. Dan, on the other hand, was a restless sleeper. He had nightmares worse than her own, and constant indigestion.

Hogben had been out hunting. When Matty went into the kitchen he was butchering a doe.

"Got a real young one, too. By accident. Couldn't see too good. There wasn't enough light."

"You forgot your glasses," said Violet. She put the meat through the grinder.

"Fawnburgers tonight," said Spaghetti Chops. Matty sat sipping her tea in silence.

"Even eaten a woman?" Hogben asked.

Matty assumed he was speaking to Spaghetti Chops who replied after a while that no, he didn't think he had.

"It's like this," Hogben began, waiting until Violet left the room for her antihistamine. "Having a regular piece of ass, or having a piece of ass and then eatin' her afterwards, well, it's like the difference between a hamburger and a hamburger deluxe."

Spaghetti Chops didn't know about that, he said. He didn't understand dogs either, especially crazy dogs like Jake.

Violet came back into the kitchen. Her allergy, Matty realized, was a reaction to her pills.

"Seen Dan and them?" Violet asked.

"No," said Matty. "Not since yesterday. I guess they went drinking again last night."

"Tsk-tsk," said Hogben. Matty watched as he cut along the doe's spine removing two thick slices of tenderloin. "She never knew what hit her," he chuckled. "She was asleep. Probably dreaming of some big buck."

Violet hissed at him. She turned to Matty. "Matty, will you go to the store," she said, fingering the ground meat. "This one was a real little skinny one. Just like you. She needs fat!"

Matty walked down to Ben's Superette. Dotty's clothesline

had blown down during the night, and there were sheets scattered from one end of the yard to the other. Dotty sat in a deck chair like a spectator at a regatta. She waved to Matty and nodded.

Matty had Jake on a leash. Jake loved going to the store because Ben Lump-Mouth would throw him the ends of the bologna that had been cut off and discarded despite the notice above the cooler saying ENDS NOT TO BE CUT OFF BALOGNA AND DISCARDED.

Ben's Superette was the only shop in the village. Ben had inherited it from his father, a sad, fat man who had walked out into the snow one winter and collapsed under his own weight. Ben's mother, a sad, thin woman, had been unable to move him. She lay down beside him, clutching at his swollen throat, and they were found that way when the snow melted, frozen together.

Ben was not a successful businessman; the shelves of the Superette were lined with the dusty remnants of his inheritance. He didn't keep fresh vegetables as tins were easier. Sometimes he had fruit but there was no demand for it. Sugar, flour, canned milk, and tea were staple purchases, a combination so frequently ordered that storekeepers in Port Atchison referred to it as "standard Indian."

Matty shouted good morning as she opened the door and the old school-bell jangled her arrival. Ben's living room, kitchen, and bedroom, which also served as a storage space for old shipments of unsaleable articles, opened out onto the store itself, and Ben sat with his back to the door watching for reflections on his portable T.V. set. Most times he missed the bell, or people didn't shout loudly enough, but when the door of the shop opened a faint image would flicker across the screen and that shadow, he knew, marked a customer.

"Anybody home?" called Matty. Jake drooled under the window where a grubby poster advertised the week's special – CHICKEN: CUT, RAPED, AND FROZEN.

"No more ends," Ben greeted her, shifting out of his

armchair to a less comfortable position behind the cash register. "Can't afford 'em these days. I get no more bologna till them ends is eaten. And not by dogs!"

"That's okay," Matty assured him. "Jake's not hungry, he's just greedy. How are you today, Ben?"

"Not gettin' any younger, that's for damn sure. I have a helluva time with my bones. Doctor says I should move to a warmer climate. What can I do for you this morning?"

"I came to see if you had any beef fat," Matty said, remembering her manners. In the Superette, unlike other stores, you were expected to ask for each item separately.

"What's that you say?" Ben said, cocking a deaf ear towards her.

"Beef fat. Pork fat will do," she repeated, as Ben adjusted his hearing aid.

"Pork and beans? Sure, I got those. They should call 'em beans with pork for all the pork that's in 'em these days. You should try Dotty's. How many tins you need?"

"Not *beans. Beef* fat. Or *pork.* No pork and beans, thank you."

When she had transportation she shopped in Port Atchison. Ultimately it was easier.

"Oh, that! Violet butcherin' again? Tell her I got a real good special on bologna ends, heh heh. Beef fat, you say? I think those damn mice were eatin' it."

"We've got mice too," Matty shouted.

"I seen 'em in here at night. They get into everything but they won't touch that margarine. No sir. I know 'cause I seen 'em steer a clear circle of the stuff. Dotty won't use it, either. She says what rats won't eat *has* to be poison. Bologna, now they'll eat that anyday. Them rascals they can even get into the cooler if they want to."

"You ought to try poison," Matty suggested.

"Raisins? No, they don't get those. Guess they ain't hungry enough. You want raisins?"

"No. But diapers. I need those disposable diapers for Baby. Have you got any?"

"Diapers! I thought you said *raisins*. If you can find 'em you're welcome to what I got. I had to clean everything out back because of them mice. But let me see now–here's a real dandy piece. You can have this one. Look all right?" He held the fat up to the light, brushing a few mice turds from the top. "Extra protein," he chuckled. "Indian medicine! You think I'm jokin', huh?"

Matty laughed politely. "Got any fruit juice today, Ben? Grannie's been asking for fruit juice."

"Prune juice? There was a coupla tins last month but I think they got bought. Dotty says some folks get blocked up before a funeral. What you want–a mixer? I think I got somethin'."

He wandered off down a dusty aisle reading aloud the labels on the tins.

"Here it is!" he said, "Hawaiian Punch. Makes you think of somewhere hot, don't it? Not like here–end of April and there's still snow in some places. The climate's changin'–it says so on the radio. Well, will you take it?"

He held out the punch. Matty could hardly refuse.

"I'll let you have it for a little less," he said. "It's been here a while."

She collected her purchases together, and Ben packed them into a used paper bag, smoothing out the creases with his wrinkled hands. He totalled the bill with the stub of a leadless pencil, scratching the figures into the brown paper so they were scarcely legible. In the old days nobody paid cash, but times had changed. Ben's New Year's resolution was to make the Superette pay and a new sign had appeared on the first of January over his old cash register:

TO TRUST IS TO BUST
TO BUST IS TO HELL

NO TRUST
NO BUST
NO HELL

Gone too were Dotty's homemade cookies and strong cups of tea laced with evaporated milk and honey. The parsnip wine had been put away with the lemon extract, and for those who had enjoyed something headier than tea, Ben's "Superette Cocktail" was no more than a fond memory.

"Two dollars and fifty-two cents even," he said. "But forget the two cents – them damn pennies just clutter up the till."

"Thanks, Ben," said Matty, edging towards the door. "I hope you'll be feeling better soon."

Ben Lump-Mouth regarded her seriously over the top of his cracked glasses. "I'm just a poor old Indian," he said. "There's nothing you can do."

11

Dan arrived home shortly before supper. His body was a mass of bruises. One eye was swollen shut and the gash on his left cheek was still bleeding. There were cuts over his brow, and the blood had matted his hair together. His clothes were torn; they smelled of urine and vomit.

Matty wouldn't listen to his excuses. She'd already heard the truth from Dorette.

Dorette had gone to Port Atchison after the funeral. She went to the beer parlour "for change." Dan was there drinking with Dickie and Rose Littleblood. Dorette joined them for a beer and they stayed until closing time. Then they went down to Henry Frog's.

Henry had whisky. They partied until they were "feeling happy." When they left Henry's, Dickie was driving. Dan had passed out in the back seat with Rose, and although Dorette was the soberest of the lot, she didn't have a licence.

Dickie had difficulty staying on the road. Swerving to avoid the centre line he sideswiped a yellow stationwagon. He drove through two stop signs and into another. He reversed into a police car.

Constable Oschinsky stepped out of the wreck. He asked to see Dickie's licence. Dickie fumbled about in the glove compartment and produced a stereo manual. The constable asked for his registration as well, and Dickie handed him a form from the Unemployment Insurance Commission saying "Your Claim Has Run Out."

The car had belonged to Noah Jones. Oschinsky shone his flashlight into the back seat enquiring, "Whom is that?" Dickie said it was his brother, Dan, who'd just come back for the funeral. He'd had a rough day, Dickie said, and shouldn't be woken.

Dorette told Matty she was praying for Dan. "I thought oh gee he's goin' to wake up and then he'll be sorry. He sure was feelin' good last night. He sure went haywire."

Dan reeked of alcohol. The constable, spotlighting Rose, demanded, "Whom is she?" Dickie said it was Rose, his cousin. He guessed she was around twenty, or twenty-one. She'd been shacked up with Noah before he drowned.

The constable asked him where they'd been that evening. Dickie said they'd been at the bar. The constable asked him how much he'd had to drink. Dickie said he didn't know, he never counted.

Dorette all the while was silent. The Mountie was young, she said. She knew him. She'd stayed with him one night after an argument with Hogben. Since then the constable had pretended she didn't exist.

He shone the light in Dan's eyes. Dan grunted and pulled the limp Rose on top of him. The light searched him out. He sat up and took a poke at it. The constable asked for his identification.

Dan told Oschinsky to fuck his hat. "Dan's been real snappy lately," said Dorette.

Dickie told Dan it was the cops. Dan pulled a case of beer from under the front seat and asked if the cops had an opener. Rose started puking. Dorette was afraid she'd choke. The constable radioed for reinforcement.

Dickie was arrested. He decided to cooperate because the constable told him that way things would go easier for him. Dan climbed out, unzipping his trousers.

"He pissed on that Mountie's car," said Dorette.

Oschinsky made a note in his little red book. Dan shouted that he wanted to be left alone. He knew his rights – this was a free country.

The paddy wagon pulled up beside him. The country might be free, said the constable, but Dan was not. He'd be all alone in the drunk tank tonight.

A squad car arrived and Dickie climbed in, sullenly. The officers hauled Rose's body out of the Firebird. Dorette said no one spoke to her until later. She was hitchhiking back to the village and the older cop gave her a ride.

"Dan wouldn't get in that wagon," Dorette said. "He was real mad. He didn't believe they were Mounties. I told him he should go with them but he didn't listen. Jeez he's stubborn. I told him, 'Watch your language!'"

Dan called Oschinsky a fat pig. Oschinsky bristled. Dan said the constable couldn't be a Mountie. "If you're a Mountie," he said, "then where's your fucking horse?"

Oschinsky prided himself on being reasonable. He wasn't given to violence either, but the night had been long and some Indians had given him trouble earlier. Dan was drunk, dangerous. Oschinsky gave him a swift knee in the groin.

Dan doubled over. A second officer tackled him from behind and sent him sprawling, head-first, on the ground. They handcuffed him and dragged him to the paddy wagon. "They sure gave him a beating," said Dorette. "Gee, they got rough."

Dan was charged with assaulting a police officer. Violet told Christian who went to bail him out.

Matty made tea while Violet fussed over Dan's face.

"I hope you don't lose that eye," she said.

Dorette said Dan would look cute with a patch.

Matty sat down with a week-old newspaper. Her hands were trembling as she thumbed through the sports pages.

Dan glanced at the headlines. "Bus fares going up," he commented.

Matty glared at him over the top of the paper. "You were

missed last night," she said, icily. "You and Dickie. You might have come–for your father's sake."

Dan sighed. "Moses never complained. I talked to him."

Doreen sniffed. "You can't talk to him," she said. "He's in heaven."

"You don't know," said Dan. "You never been there."

"Neither have you," said Doreen, "so how come you heard him talking?"

Matty closed her eyes. The voices became specks of white light dancing under her eyelids. She had moved into her own house of silence. She looked out from it now with grave calm.

It was dusty in there and breathing was difficult. She could see Dan crouching in a far corner, wearing a mask. Not the Wild Man of the Woods she'd once imagined but a death mask carved from cedar. There were two holes for eyes, a hole each for the nose and mouth, and it was painted a ghostly white.

When her voice came it was a whisper without pitch or stress. She knew it was time.

"I want to go," she said.

She couldn't see his face. He held his hands shut as though he were trying to grasp something that was slipping away from him.

He forced a laugh. "Are you crazy? Where would you go? Look–I'm staying home tonight, okay? I won't go anywhere."

She moved towards him. He could touch her now. He lowered the mask, and in places where his skin was scraped she could see the bone. His lips were glazed with blisters. She kissed him and he began to bleed. His arms closed around her. He clawed at her continually like an annoying hurt.

She pulled away. He dug and scratched at his swollen eye. She couldn't look, couldn't stand the pain that lived in him. His blood was all colours, bubbles of colour that burst open and spilled over his face.

She opened her eyes and the world turned grey. Dan's face was framed by the greyness, his good eye leaden and filled with a child's sadness. She preferred the colours inside her head.

"We can't," she said, "it's no good, I can't live with you."

Dan took a deep breath. "Jesus, you're crazy! All this because I missed one lousy dinner!"

She folded the newspaper and placed it on the table. Violet and the twins had left the room.

"It's no use, Dan. I want to go – really." Her words came weakly now, falling off at the ends.

"Then fuck yourself," Dan said. He spat to clear his throat, then threw back his head. "If you don't like the way things are – and I told you before – then go. Go fuck a white-man. Fuck yourself!"

Jake was lying on a fishnet that smelled of a recent catch. He stood up, shook his head, and hobbled towards the door. Dan grabbed Spaghetti Chops's skinning knife and hurled it after the dog. The knife sank into the wall, missing him by inches.

Jake dodged the toaster and the electric frying pan before escaping into the cupboard. Matty ducked under the sink to avoid the sugar bowl and the Chewable Vitamin C Tablets. She surveyed her own weaponry: a box of S.O.S., a spray-can of Raid and Mr. Muscle Self-Scouring Overnight Oven Cleaner. The very names of the products suggested warfare but she had no time now to consider tactics.

Dan had punched his way out of the kitchen door and was reaching for the axe when Doreen and Dorette came squawking to Matty's rescue. Dorette wrestled with the axe while Doreen attacked Dan with the newspaper. Matty escaped and locked herself in the bathroom; Dan got away in the pickup. The twins, their squawks subsiding into squeals, began to reassemble the shambles.

When the house was quiet again, Matty crept out of the

bathroom. She packed her bags and tiptoed downstairs. Christian was sitting at the kitchen table. He'd already heard the whole story from Doreen.

Matty told him she was going to East Oyster. "I've got to go back," she said, "only to get my things. I'm going to write to my father. He'll lend me some money until I'm settled. I don't know what I'm going to do. I can't think about it."

Christian was going fishing again. At the end of the month he was driving to Squinskut to borrow a boat from Archie Seeweed. Archie had a trapline somewhere up the Kisgula. Christian said it was ten days by canoe and another day's hike inland.

"I went there as a boy," he said, "a couple of times with Uncle Archie. I'm going to build a new cabin and work his traps. You're welcome to come along if you like. You should come for the summer. You know the Kisgula?"

"I've heard of it," said Matty, remembering a recent newscast. Victims of a plane crash had been discovered without heads, and a crew of investigative journalists found other skeletons, similarly decapitated, in the same area. "Doesn't the Kisgula flow through the Headless Valley?"

Christian smiled. "It does," he said, "but much farther north. We don't have headhunters in this part of the country. The Indians down here are civilized!"

Part Three
The Kisgula

12

Matty drove back alone from Old Mystic. Dan had tried to stop her. He tried pleading with her, he tried using threats. But this time there was nothing that would make her decide to stay.

She had nothing to say to him. "I'm tired, Dan," she said.

Dan only looked at her but she knew what his body said. "I'm tired, too, but not the way you are."

Christian told Dan to hang on until his trial. Matty was going to clean out the trailer and wait for Christian to join her. She'd decided to go north with him where she could think things over. Dan sat slumped at the table, registering nothing.

It was drizzling as Matty pulled into East Oyster. The sun was trying to shine in the western sky and Bette Millar was in her front yard adjusting her T.V. antenna.

Matty stopped for coffee. Bette said they'd had power outages since Saturday due to the heavy gale. Her seventy-foot T.V. antenna was damaged and she'd been without her favourite T.V. programs for nearly a week. Bette also told Matty that they had new neighbours. "They're worth getting to know," she said, "and check the size of their screen."

Bette gave Matty all the camp gossip. The mail had been late twice and the Coopers had a German visiting. Angie Ward had the misfortune to fall down the stairs and injure a leg. Limping around didn't appeal to her.

Matty told Bette she had left Dan. She knew there'd be no need to tell anyone else.

"Just don't end up in the drink like what's-her-name," Bette warned her. "You know, Albert's Harriet. There's plenty of fish in the sea. You don't need to mess around with natives. You love them and what do you get? Deep down they hate our guts."

Matty told Bette her plans as they walked to the car. The sun was going down behind the hills and a light rain was misting the air. Bette pointed at the rainbow. She thought the sunset would make an interesting painting.

The trailer felt abandoned the moment Matty entered it. She slung her coat over Dan's buckskin vest. The vest hung like Dan's body, and she didn't want the reminder.

The sheets on their bed smelled musty. She made herself a snack and curled up on the chesterfield with a book. The trailer was damp, comfortless. She wouldn't stay any longer than necessary; she could wait for Christian at the hotel in Onanuga.

She drifted into sleep. The trees formed a canopy over her head and she was walking, lost, her arms filled with books and papers.

There was a river – she imagined it was the Kisgula. It was midnight and there was a rainbow. Dan floated towards her in a coffin-shaped canoe.

He looked like a spirit. He had woven roots into bracelets and wrapped them around his arms. He wore a vest made from cedar bark and a feathered headdress. His eyes looked out from deep inside his head and he had painted large charcoal circles around them.

He was dead, he told her; he was an angel. If she didn't believe him she would never wake up.

She wanted to stop dreaming. The river was rising and her papers were getting wet. The jungle was full of angels. She could hear them chanting, filling her head with visions.

She felt dizzy. She tried to run away. She dropped her

books but Dan took her hands and bound them with roots. She was too tired to struggle, and the light from the rainbow sent a coldness sweeping through her.

She didn't believe in angels. The jungle hissed. Dan had vanished and all around her there were black-spiked flowers. Their tongues flicked out at her like quick green snakes.

They licked her head until there was nothing left. She needed her head: she couldn't wake up without it. She couldn't see or think or talk or listen. Her head was in heaven, was in darkness with the angels.

She woke up, hours later, with a stiff neck. She'd thrashed about in her sleeping bag all night and every muscle in her body was aching.

The telephone rang. It was Bette Millar. Elfie, their new neighbour, was dying to have coffee.

Matty went back to sleep. She didn't dream again. When she woke up it was after three o'clock. The sun was shining in her face.

She got dressed and went outside, annoyed with herself for having wasted the day. Elfie Wells hailed her from across the fence, and Matty went over for coffee, taking a bunch of carnations. The flowers were left over from Moses Seeweed's funeral: Violet had given her the non-plastic arrangements because they would die on the grave and spoil the look of it.

Elfie thought the gift was "genuinely honest-to-goodness touching" but she couldn't have carnations in the house because of Rocky, her husband, who was allergic to nature.

"How does he manage, working in the bush?" Matty asked.

"Pills," Elfie confided over a cup of hot Postum. "He takes them regular. They upset his stomach, though. He can't keep a cup of coffee down. I send him to work without a thermos."

She sighed. Matty shook her head sympathetically.

"I tell you, it's some racket those doctors have going for them. Rocky he can't live without them now–pills. It's a real genuine shame. That lady doctor thingamabob–you know the one I mean–from the old country–well, they tell me this is her first practice. That's what she's doing all right. Practising. *Rocky is allergic to nature*, she says to me. I says to her, *you gotta be kidding.*

"When we first got hitched, Rocky and me, he wasn't allergic like this. But with all these doctors practising and experimenting they're turning him into a real honest-to-goodness hypochondriac. We come from Rocky Mountain House, eh, and that's where it first started. The reaction, that is. I thought I might have put too much fabric softener in the wash. I've heard that can do it. Now I wash his shirts separate. It's not easy living this far from a laundromat."

Matty frowned. "Wouldn't he be better off working in an office?"

"That would kill him. Besides, you can't escape from nature. It's all the rage to have plants in offices these days. Even that doctor has some. You can't just chuck them out the window when you feel one coming on–an attack, eh. Sure, he has attacks. It's a real shame–it's not normal. And Rocky, he's the outdoor type. I says to him, *Rocky, listen to me! Stay inside why don't you. You'll live longer.* But does he listen? *I wear the pants in this family* he says.

"He shouldn't go outside if he's allergic to nature," Matty continued, weakly. The conversation was going in circles.

"Long's he takes his pills," Elfie repeated, "*and* watches his diet. I can't get him to eat vegetables. Cauliflower, that's the worst. He breaks out in boils, and when those boils start to pop, boy, you gotta move fast. And Rocky he gets infected real easy."

Matty realized she'd made a mistake bringing the flowers. She'd felt lonely in the trailer, surrounded by her past, but she returned to start packing with a new sense of purpose.

She'd made a mistake, too, spending four years of her life in the logging camp at East Oyster. "What's the matter with it?" Dan had argued. "The pay's no better anywheres else."

She remembered the story of a Zen monk who'd lived alone on a mountaintop trying to find the Truth. After thirty-nine years he came down from the mountain. The truth was he had wasted his time.

Now I can see the road
To the highway;
The road that carries us away . . .

All is changed now
I'm not running
But going home
With my pa
Oh God

"Evolutionary Obsequies" by Martha Clarke, aged thirteen, had been published in her high-school annual. She'd never fully understood the title herself but the poem had sentimental value: she'd written it after she'd run away from home.

Pink blossom
And a seagull
We must be getting
close to
prison . . . (home)

Matty had taken her grandmother's coin collection to buy food, and it was three days before a private detective found her crouched beside the railway tracks composing those lines. Matty had kept all her old poems, thinking they might mean something one day, but now they seemed embarrassingly clear and she put them aside to be burned.

It took her several weeks to pack up and clean the trailer. She spent an afternoon sorting through old family photographs, saving one of her mother looking elegant in velvet and one of her father looking restless in a rented tux. She found a faded portrait by a hack in a studio, an ill-defined image of herself and Dan united.

Bette offered to store her belongings. She advised Matty to burn the furniture to stop Dan from having the satisfaction.

"You know how they get," she said, "and besides he'll probably bring some squaw with him. If I were you I'd get rid of those appliances. Take them to the dump. That'll teach him!"

Bette's husband–"Merv, he's a genius"–inspected Matty's car. The Heap had been a birthday present from Dan, and though Matty seldom drove it there was, according to Merv, "life in the old girl yet." He checked the oil and filled the gas tank. The Heap was out of gas, he explained, and that's why she hadn't been running.

When the car was ready, Matty drove to the post office. She'd written to Christian to say she was moving, but there was no reply. She left a forwarding address with the postmistress and collected her mail. A parcel from the Open Shelf Library in Victoria had arrived with a covering note explaining that one book she had ordered was currently on loan but that another of a similar interest had been substituted. *The Edible Woman* was replaced by a vegetarian cookbook.

There was also a letter from her father. It contained a "small cheque" and a photograph of himself looking nautical.

My dear Martha:

I am hoping this will reach you before you embark on your travels. I am sending a small cheque to tide you over the next month or so. There will be more later if you need it and when you have decided on a course for the future. Naturally your aunt and I are concerned about you at the moment. However, as you suggest, it may prove to be a valuable experience in the long run.

Dot and I went sailing last weekend with some old

friends from San Francisco and their grandchildren. California in May is a longshot nicer than where you are, weatherwise. I hope you have enough warm gear. You know how I worry about your health!

Anyway, I started to tell you about the sailing trip. It was quite fun on the whole but it was not easy to cater to the kids' dislikes in the way of meals. None of them liked salads so we had to rely on fruit and canned foods once we had finished a ham and a chicken we started out with. Dot was feeling a bit under the weather. She has managed to stay off the Valium ever since and is, at the moment, making excellent progress. She is currently attending a Bible Seminar in Sacramento. Well, if it gives her courage I don't see the harm in it.

I hope you will come and see us in the fall. I am getting to be an old man. The people on the television all talk about the energy crisis – I am experiencing one myself these days.

I trust you are well and feeding yourself properly. You have survived so well, so far.

Take care of yourself, and Happy Landings!

Your Affectionate Dad.

Matty said her good-byes to East Oyster. She drove into Onanuga and took a room at the Terminal Hotel.

The room was small. The chesterfield and chairs had been recovered in lime and the chenille bedspread, dyed yellow to soften the stains, had been thrown back to conceal a large burn in the bedstead where a previous occupant had tried to start a fire.

Matty lay down with Gideon's Bible. Flies clustered around the naked lightbulb that hung from a hole in the ceiling. On the cigarette-scarred night table there was a telephone and a small notice: "Lonely? In Despair? *Somebody* cares" – and the number of Suicides Anonymous.

She took a second look; she was imagining things. It was

simply an inducement by the telephone company to "Call Home Tonight."

She switched off the light. She couldn't sleep. The pipes groaned in the bathroom where the water dripped brown from the tap, and through the walls she could hear the bass-line from the beer parlour juke-box.

Outside it was raining. From the window, which didn't open, Matty had a view of the Public Health Clinic. She got dressed again and went downstairs. Joe Garcia, a hooktender from East Oyster, bought her a Harvey Wallbanger.

There were two Indian women at the next table; one of them was smoking a cigar. She began to cough violently and the ash fell off into her beer. Her friend was struggling with a can of sardines. She wrenched it open with her nailfile and fish oil oozed onto her tangerine-coloured stretch pants.

"You know what they say about squaws," Joe said. "They got T.B. or they got V.D. If they cough, you can fuck 'em."

When the cabaret closed, he left with the one who smoked. Matty went to the bathroom where the words SHOOT A WHITEMAN IN THE BALLS had been smeared in blood on the cubicle door. Below, in red lipstick, someone had retaliated. SHOOT AN INDIAN IN THE BRAINS, IT'LL DO LESS DAMAGE.

13

The week passed slowly. Every day Matty slept late into the morning before going downstairs for a beer and a sandwich. She read the Bible, the *Oracle*, two Harlequin romances, and her library books. She watched television, played Patience; she knitted half a scarf. Christian was due to arrive on Sunday. On Saturday she went to the Food Giant.

Angie Ward was doing her weekly shopping.

"How you doing, doll?" she chirped over the produce. "Anything new or strange?"

Matty stuck her finger into an overripe tomato.

"Haven't you heard? I'm leaving."

"I heard," said Angie, "but I didn't believe it. So it's for real. I mean, you're pulling out? I can't say I blame you – it's no life. Bette tells me you got a new boyfriend. So what's he like?"

"He's a friend," said Matty. "I went to school with him. We're going up the Kisgula tu build a cabin. After that, I don't know what."

"The Kisgula! Bette told me. I thought she was joking! What are you going to eat – berries? What if you get sick? There's no hospital."

"There's nothing," said Matty. "I guess Christian will go hunting. I'm taking a few supplies with us. Can you think of anything?"

"Spices," said Angie, emphatically, "for variety. When the meat goes off you just toss in a handful of curry powder. Here – Nabob – it's the cheapest. You're not paying for a fancy label."

Angie dropped a large tin of curry powder into Matty's basket. Matty smiled, thinking of her grandfather, and she told Angie the story.

Her grandfather had been in the British Army, stationed in Malaya. He and his men got stranded in the jungle; they had to live on roots until a rescue plane found them. It circled twice and then disappeared. Later it returned and dropped a food parcel containing twenty pounds of curry powder.

"Terrific," said Angie, "but this ain't Malaya, kid. Take some – you'll thank me for it. What else's on your list?"

She read aloud over Matty's shoulder. "You've forgotten Tampax – and bum-wipe! There's a special on today, but don't buy it. It's that crummy stuff. Like sandpaper."

They pushed on to the dairy products. Angie kept up an inane chatter until Matty could no longer concentrate. She retreated into a dim jungle world where everything seemed soft and yellow, like butter. Her shopping basket, she thought, smelled rotten.

She felt feverish, too.

"You look sick," said Angie. "Are you feeling all right?"

Matty looked at Angie. Her face was the colour of thick custard.

Angie took her hand. "Are you all right? Shall I get somebody?"

Matty shook her head. She bent down over her basket and closed her eyes. Her basket was full of oranges; a strong fruity odour replaced the smell of rot, and when she opened her eyes again, the jungle had vanished.

"You should go to bed," said Angie. "You look tired. Get some rest."

Matty nodded. She studied her shopping list; she could read each word clearly. It worried her that she drifted away so easily. Her dreaming had become a habit that was no longer confined to sleep.

"Stress," said Angie, "it's a killer. You're probably not eating properly, either. Why don't you let me cook you a meal?"

Matty shook her head again. She thanked Angie for the invitation, but declined. Last time she'd gone round for a meal she'd found Angie soaking in the tub and dinner drying in the oven. She'd spent the whole evening feeling uncomfortable while Angie complained about her sex life.

"Well, come over and visit, eh? Any time except Wednesday. That's Bud's night off. Fuck Night he calls it."

Matty told her it would depend on Christian.

"You need to relax, kid," said Angie. "Get out more, play the field."

That evening Matty had egg rolls at the Wigwam Café She lost a game of pool to Joe Garcia and Joe bought her a drink.

"They're good in bed because they don't care what happens," he said, turning the conversation to Indian women. "You don't have to feel guilty or talk to them or nothing."

Matty, after several more drinks, asked Joe to spend the night with her.

"You're Dan's problem," he said, tersely. "I don't go looking for trouble."

Sunday came and went. There was no sign of Christian. On Thursday night he arrived. Dan was with him. Matty's anxiety turned to fear.

Dan had a handcuff dangling from his wrist. The wounds on his face had reopened and Matty felt sick. He was drunk, he said he loved her, he wasn't leaving without her. Matty reached for the telephone to call the RCMP.

Christian stopped her. He checked Dan into another room and made him promise to stay there.

"He jumped bail last week," Christian told her. "They

picked him up on Monday. That's why I'm late. I was trying to sort things out. They were taking him down to Vancouver last night and he managed to give them the slip. He's lucky he didn't get hurt."

Matty refused to see him.

"He's been crazy since you left," said Christian. "I told him it wouldn't do any good, but I had to bring him to see you. He wants to come up north with us. I told him we'd have to think about it."

Matty was furious. Their plans were ruined. She imagined having to hide from the law, or worse, being charged with harbouring a criminal.

"He's still your husband," said Christian, "and he's my brother. We can't just abandon him. We've got to do something."

The hotel was like a prison. Matty could hear Dan pacing up and down in the next room. Christian took him something to eat and found him forcing the window. Dan wanted a gun. He started beating on the wall, and Christian couldn't restrain him.

It was ten-thirty. Matty went downstairs. The bar was full of half-drunk loggers; she left the hotel. She could hear Dan shouting as she passed beneath his window. He wanted to kill someone. She walked.

She walked quickly. The town had taken on the appearance of an enemy, had closed itself against her. The Wigwam Café was empty, the laundromat shut due to an outbreak of scabies. The bank, post office, and government buildings were locked up tight and there was a stag party ("for male members only") at the Canadian Legion Hall. Only the RCMP station showed signs of life. She stood in the darkness, her heart pounding.

The detachment was well lit; she could see somebody working. From the hotel she could hear the juke-box that never stopped playing. She struggled with herself, weighing the alternatives. The light was drawing her. It was the only solution.

She tapped on the door and the man looked up from his desk. He yawned and scratched his armpit. A key chain dangled from the handcuff at his waist.

He was wearing a T-shirt and a pair of dark trousers. She tapped again and he stood up, stretching. A feeling of relief swept through her as she watched him walk towards her. Compressed into each movement was the accumulated knowledge of his power.

He unlocked the door. He motioned her inside and showed her to his desk. She sat down while he poured her a cup of black coffee. She could no longer hear the juke-box, but a new rhythm, a sad dull sound, filled her head.

There were photographs on the wall: a car accident and the automobile graveyard. A wrecked Chevelle mounting a two-ton pickup had been inscribed with the message WELCOME HOME CRIME. Matty told the constable her story. He listened to her without interrupting.

Afterwards he drove her to Angie Ward's. Angie, without asking questions, gave her a bed for the night. In the morning, after a bath and a light breakfast, Matty walked back into town.

It was almost noon. She bought an *Oracle* but there was no news. She went upstairs; when she knocked on Dan's door there was no answer. She knocked again to make quite sure. The room was empty.

Christian was lying on her bed. "He's gone," he said, as Matty looked at him questioningly. "Last night, around midnight. While I was out looking for you."

She couldn't tell him the truth. She said she'd been visiting Angie and had decided to spend the night. Christian stopped listening in the middle of her story, stood up, and looked off through the window as if she weren't there, as if he hadn't believed her.

"Are you sure he got away?" Matty asked, confused. "What are we going to do?"

Christian shrugged. "He broke down the door," he said. "It's really my fault. I shouldn't have left him."

He lay back on the bed and closed his eyes. "I looked everywhere. He's gone."

The twice-weekly freight train from Gateway thundered by and Dan's empty beer bottles rattled in their cases.

"What are we going to do?" said Matty, as the train passed, echoing.

"Cash in those empties," said Christian.

14

They left Onanuga early in the evening. The road, in places, was barely recognizable. Winter rains had eroded the banks and at one point they found themselves driving along a river bed. At dusk, with two smashed headlights, they beached the Heap. They found a sheltered spot at the edge of the woods and pitched their tent on higher ground.

All night the rain dripped on the canvas.

"There's a mosquito," Matty whispered. She poked Christian who sat up, fumbling for his flashlight. He switched it on, shining it at Matty.

The mosquito landed on her arm and she pulled her skin tight around it.

"Don't move," she said, "I've got him!"

The mosquito filled up with blood, and burst. Christian made a face and turned off the light.

Matty wiped the blood on her sleeping bag.

"That's the one useful thing I learned at summer camp," she said. "The proboscis gets stuck. They can't stop sucking."

"I saw," said Christian. "If you ignore them, they won't bother you."

"Dan says it's my skin," said Matty, "that I have a different smell than most people. We'd be out in the bush, he'd never get bitten!"

"They don't like dark meat," said Christian. "Go back to sleep. It's early."

"I can't," said Matty. "I've been having a nightmare."

She and Dan were living in a little shack. It was the middle of winter and the middle of nowhere and they were running out of food. Christian came to visit one night and Dan murdered him. He did it, he said, so they could eat.

Matty was afraid someone would recognize the body. Dan skinned it and cut it into bits. He moulded the pieces into the shape of a small animal, covered it with hide and put it in the fridge. "Now it's just meat," he said. But Matty knew it was Christian.

"Tent's leaking," said Christian, covering his head with his raincoat. "What time is it, about?"

Matty stuck her head out through the tent flaps. "It's starting to get light," she said.

Christian went fishing. He caught a trout which they ate for breakfast along with stale doughnuts from the Food Giant and soda crackers stuck together with peanut butter. Matty made tea.

A cold wind was blowing across the valley.

"We should make Squinskut in another four hours if the road doesn't get any worse," said Christian. Rain blew into the fire and hissed on the rocks. "It's nice country but we won't see much if this weather keeps up.

"It's easy to get lost out here," he added. "You could disappear forever if you wanted to. It wouldn't even matter if we did disappear. No one would miss us anyway."

Matty huddled closer to the fire. She kept seeing Dan's face in the coals, wounded the way it looked the last time she saw him.

Dan would miss her. She wished she knew for certain where he was. If he hadn't gone to jail he'd be sure to come looking for her. Christian had told him where they were going and in all likelihood he would get there first.

The rain was drowning their fire. They broke camp and

packed the car. When they set off across the valley they were driving into the wind. The Heap strained against the force and Matty sat silently, her face pressed against the glass.

They were following a river. To the east the country was a succession of swamp-barrens covered with small bull pines and occasional cedars. A forest fire had ravaged the area years earlier and a few solitary snags pointed like charred fingers into the sky. Fireweed and daisies filled the ditches. Burned-out stumps like fat black bears dotted the landscape. A flock of kinglets rose out of the lichen-moss.

"I came here with Archie once, bearhunting," said Christian, as if he knew what she was thinking. "I shot a stump. Archie says that bears have supernatural power. They can change themselves into stumps the moment they see us coming."

Mountain ranges, capped with snow, flanked the valley on both sides, receding into the distance. The shades of colour varied from the snowline downwards, the blue and purple of the mountains showing above the dark green of spruce and cedar, changing to the lighter green of the cottonwood and yellow on the lower reaches of the valley. To the west a great lava plain stretched to the foot of the mountains, and Matty saw signs–sections of trees and roots, the wood still in good preservation, were partly encrusted with the lava–indicating its recent origin.

"The river didn't always flow this way," said Christian. "It flowed along by the base of the mountains on the west side of the valley. Archie told me the eruption occurred when his grandfather was a boy. Some people were camped there when the spirits of the mountain got angry."

The Indians were all busy, Christian said, preparing salmon to smoke for the winter. Some young boys were amusing themselves by catching salmon and cutting openings in their backs, in which they inserted long narrow stones from the river bottom. They set the salmon free and stood back laughing. The salmon swam near the surface of the water; the boys clapped their hands and called them finback whales.

Meanwhile the ground began to tremble. Suddenly one of the mountains erupted and the fire-stone began flowing down. The Indians fled, and at sunset, as they looked back, they saw a spirit-cloud, its fiery wings outspread, following them. They reached the foothills on the other side of the valley, and there took refuge in the mountains.

The flow of fire-stone, swept on by the cloud-spirit, drove the river across the valley. By the time it had reached the middle of the valley, the river had cooled the lava leaving the plain behind it.

"According to legend, it was all because of those boys," said Christian, "because of their cruel treatment of the salmon. Archie called it 'mischief.' There's no word for cruelty in the Indian language."

The road swung sharply to the left and they crossed the river on a plank bridge. They climbed steadily until they were driving through thick forest under the slope of the mountains. The rain grew heavier. The Heap seemed reluctant to continue and died several times before Christian could coax life into it.

They climbed higher and higher. The mountains made Matty think of postcard reproductions: they were "majestic" and "awe-inspiring" and "breathtakingly beautiful." They were also monotonous.

"Do these mountains have a name?" she asked. "Are you sure we're going the right way?"

"It's the only way," said Christian. "The Indians call it the Squingaany–Place-Where-There-Is-No-Reason-To-Be. On the map they're called the Baldwin Range. They're named after a U.S. Navy pilot who crashed into one of the peaks."

The road rose before them, a sequence of treacherous rocky ledges. The hairpin curves wound towards inaccessible slopes and windy plateaus. The rain turned to sleet; the windshield wipers jammed. An eagle appeared out of the clouds, soared along beside them, then dived. Matty dared not look over the plunging edges.

And then they were descending. Christian had to fight to keep the car on the road, swerving to avoid dislodged boulders and the deep ruts where water had cut right down to bedrock. In other places there were mud holes over a foot deep. A falling rock shattered the cracked windshield.

"I can't see. Roll down your window!" he shouted, as the car shuddered towards a cliff.

"The oil light's come on," cried Matty. She opened her window and was immediately splattered with mud.

Christian manoeuvred the car back onto a straight course. "I checked the oil before we left," he said, "but that's the least of our worries. I think we're going to make it! Hang on, we've nearly hit bottom!"

The road levelled and they were driving through dense timber again. Christian stopped to push out the windshield; they'd lost their muffler and the radiator was leaking. Further along a sound like chains being dragged over a cattle-grid issued from the bowels of the car; they exchanged anxious glances and continued in silence. Further still, where the forest dwindled into second-growth timber that was rapidly being choked out by renegade alder, the Heap ground to a halt.

"Now what?" Matty cried, as the car shook in a final spasm. "What are we going to do now?"

"Walk," said Christian. "What else do you suggest? If your speedometer was accurate we're only about ten miles from the village."

"What about the car?" asked Matty, alarmed. "Can't you fix it? Maybe we've run out of oil. Just check it."

"It's got nothing to do with the oil," said Christian. He made a cursory inspection, lying on his back in the mud. "It's the transmission – but that's only part of the problem. We're lucky we made it this far. I can't do much. It's too rusty."

The floor under the back seat was gone and the Heap had been taking on water. Two bags of wet flour had to be discarded.

"Let's start unloading," said Christian, "before anything else gets ruined."

They emptied the car and pushed it off the road. Christian made a shelter for their supplies and then set off to explore.

Matty was collecting pitchwood for a fire when the Heap subsided into its final resting place, crushing the bank of cowparsley. She'd never been able to understand machinery, but now the Heap looked hurt, full of spectral personality.

"You're projecting," said Christian, when he returned moments later. "You're tired. You need to eat something. Squinskut, by the way, is just around the bend."

15

The sun had come out; Matty squinted through the unaccustomed brightness. The road stopped at a washed-out bridge. The bank had collapsed on the far side of the river, and a garbage dump was being carried away downstream. A waterlogged mattress was pinned against an old piling, and a sandbar was forming where the river altered its course. A handpainted sign beyond the submerged bridge announced VILLAGE OF SQUINSKUT. YOUR WELCOME.

"Is Archie expecting us?" called Matty as they scrambled down the bank and crossed the river on a slippery log protruding from the sandbar.

"I wrote to Aunt Lou," Christian called back, "but I don't know whether she got the letter. I know where they live, anyway. You can't miss it: there're only ten houses in the whole village."

But in the fifteen years Christian had been away Squinskut's population had more than doubled. Two dozen tarpapered shacks lined the main and only street.

The street was deserted. The flag was flying at half-mast over the boarded-up schoolhouse, not because anybody had died recently but because no one had ever bothered to raise it any farther. Fire had gutted the church and the graveyard. Charred tombstones lay scattered over the ground.

"Creepy, isn't it?" said Matty, taking in the whole town at

a glance. "I get the feeling nobody lives here."

"There's Archie's place," said Christian. "The one with the roof!"

He pointed to a half-completed shack propped between the crumbling shells of two hovels. A rickety ladder minus several rungs replaced the steps; the front door was missing and a blanket covered the hole.

Christian risked the ladder and Matty climbed after him, stepping around a battered highchair filled with broken toys and tripping over an old dog who no longer cared.

Archie Seeweed was asleep on the chesterfield, a bottle of beer full of drowned cigarette butts in one hand. He had slept in the same spot for years and had never changed his clothes. His shoes had worn deep holes in the chesterfield and, like thick, sweaty rats, his feet nested there.

The television lay face down in the middle of the room, small wires issuing like veins from its cold heart. In the bedroom a wartime play was raging on the radio.

Christian gave Archie a shake.

"Uncle Archie! Wake up! It's me, Christian!"

The old man grunted and shifted his weight from one side to the other. He opened his sunken eyes for an instant.

"Where's Aunt Lou and the kids? Who's looking after this place?"

The eyes closed again, hoarding their secrets. "Gone." He scratched his genitals and coughed up a mouthful of phlegm. He spat. "That woman's never coming back. She's gone. Give me a drink."

"She's probably gone to Vancouver," Christian said, turning to Matty. "Violet told me their eldest daughter is living down there and Lou likes to visit the grandchildren."

He took Uncle Archie's hand. "How long has the weather been like this, Uncle Archie? The bridge has fallen down. Did you know that?"

Matty surveyed the room feeling sick to her stomach. Dirty

dishes and pee-stained underwear lay heaped under half-eaten tins of cat food.

"Uncle Archie? I want you to meet my friend Matty. She's right here. Look. Behind you. We're going to stay in your cabin for the summer. Remember your cabin way up the river? Remember when you and I used to go there?"

Archie shook his head.

"Matty is Dan's wife. You remember Dan-Boy, don't you. Matty and I are going to work your trapline. I guess you haven't been up there for awhile, eh?"

"Gone," Archie mumbled. "Give me a drink." He looked around, his eyes slowly focusing. "Who's that?" he asked hoarsely, indicating Matty.

"Matty. She was married to Dan. Dan's wife. Now tell me, where's Aunt Lou?"

"I loved my wife," said Archie. "I loved her."

"I know. Where is she?"

"Gone," he shrugged. "She broke my heart."

"Why don't you make him a cup of tea," Christian said to Matty. "Like a cup of tea, Uncle Archie?"

The old man nodded. He buried his face in his hands.

Matty went into the kitchen. There was no tea, only stale beer under the sink and rusty tap water. In the fridge there were more tins of cat food.

"What happened to the T.V. set?" she heard Christian asking.

"Broke," Archie repeated. "She broke my heart. I'm dying."

"No, you're not," said Christian. "When did you last have anything to eat?"

"Give me a drink. I only want to live," said Archie.

Christian joined Matty in the kitchen. "He's in pretty rough shape," he said. "Isn't there anything to eat besides cat food?"

"Nothing," replied Matty. "Only what we've got in our

packs. What are we going to do with him? We can't just leave him here."

"I know," said Christian. "We'll get one of the neighbours. First he's got to eat something. See what you can find. I'm going to talk to him about the boat."

Matty produced the dried halibut; Archie couldn't chew it. He only wanted a drink, he said. Matty made weak cocoa while Christian questioned him in the living room.

"He says the boat's gone too. Somebody borrowed it. Took it to go fishing and never brought it back. That's the only sense I can make out of him. He thinks Aunt Lou left because of the television."

"What next?" Matty asked, wearily. "We've got no car and no boat. I suppose that means we'll stay *here* all summer."

"I saw a canoe behind the schoolhouse," said Christian. "Not exactly a *whole* canoe, but I might be able to mend it. It's worth a try."

They camped beside the river. Christian made several trips back for their belongings while Matty cooked supper and finished off the rum. Christian sucked on the dried halibut and Matty roasted small chunks of cheese. They had chocolate for dessert and some beer nuts that Christian found in the lining of his jacket.

The next day Christian rose early to make enquiries in the village. The canoe belonged to one Sampson Sam–he'd bought it from a mail-order catalogue. It had arrived in two pieces and no one had figured out how to assemble it. Christian managed, with the help of a young boy named Sasquatch, to put the canoe together.

No one knew where Aunt Lou had gone. Christian arranged for a woman to stay with Uncle Archie until Lou returned or Archie died, whichever happened first. Cordelia Sam, who lived three doors down, said she'd be glad of the company since Sampson was away fishing. Cordelia moved into the bedroom with the radio. Archie sank deeper into the chesterfield.

Cordelia's daughter operated a small grocery store from the kitchen of her house. Matty went to buy flour but the store was empty. Cordelia's daughter explained that the supply truck was a month overdue. There was no way of getting a message out with the bridge down.

Sasquatch helped Christian load the canoe. The boy wanted to know where they were going and why they were going and how long they would be staying and if he could come with them. He dragged his club foot along the muddy bank, calling after them for gum-chewy, tobacco, and hootchinoo.

"I'm not giving him anything," said Christian. "He's already picked my wallet."

Matty paddled until her arms grew sore. She sat in the bow of the canoe watching the world slip past. The river was still, the image of the river bank perfectly reflected. Occasionally a patch of alder broke the symmetry, or a delicate cedar dipping its feathery branches. As the shadows lengthened the deer came to feed in the water meadows.

Christian beached the canoe before dark. Numerous bear trails had been beaten into the soft ground, and everywhere near the river there was fresh bear dung. The woods were full of ravens. Christian shot a mallard that was feeding on the flats.

The days passed quickly and the weather grew warmer. At night, when the wind had died, there were mosquitoes. Christian would pitch the tent then crawl inside to kill all that had entered. But Matty couldn't sleep. The buzz of mosquitoes rose and fell as they surrounded the tent like killer bees, seeking an entrance.

In the morning Christian would build up the fire. He

scraped together the hot cinders and piled on the green alder. Matty would stand in the smoke with closed eyes and mouth, content to gasp occasionally for a mouthful of air. A cup of tea, which she held in one hand, and a cedar bough, which she grasped in the other to beat off her assailants, would prepare her for another day.

They paddled for two weeks. The rapids marked the end of their voyage; on their last night Christian shot a buck. Matty devised a headnet out of cheesecloth, fastening it around her hat brim. She worked late into the evening, preparing the deerskin.

Using the inner bone of the deer's foreleg, she scraped off the hair and grain. She boiled the liver, added tree-moss and brains she had squeezed through her fingers, and shaped the mash into a cake of soap. When dried in this form the brain would keep indefinitely. Matty planned to make buckskin when they reached Archie's shack, and the brain-mash – the cake dissolved in hot water and the moss removed – would be used for tanning.

When the skin was clean she rubbed it with bacon grease. She stored it, rolled up, under her seat in the canoe.

Approaching the rapids the river began to grow narrower. In order to steer clear of the great eddies which opened on every side threatening to engulf them, they had to keep a strong headway on the canoe.

High spurs of rock jutted out from either side of the bank leaving a small passageway. They put in at a beach on the eastern shore; the sun was high, a brisk wind keeping away the mosquitoes. They unloaded the canoe and carried it into the woods. Christian cached their supplies.

That evening they went fishing. Climbing over the rocky outcrop, they descended on the other side of the gap where the river widened forming a series of rapids and cataracts. They walked for an hour before the flooding waters prevented them from continuing any further. Matty turned back to set up camp. Christian followed slowly, stopping to cast for trout in the deep moss-coloured pools.

He returned at dusk, empty-handed.

"Not a bite," he said, "they weren't even curious." He stopped, seeing the look on Matty's face.

"Our canoe's gone," she said.

16

"There's been a fire here recently," said Christian. Bark had been stripped from an uprooted cedar, a small supply of dry kindling stored in a sheltered place under the root's overhang.

"Who do you think it is?" Matty whispered, immediately conjuring up images of headhunters. They could be watching them even now; she tossed her head, flicking her hair out of her eyes. She and Christian would make valuable trophies. Fair hair, she knew, was greatly prized.

"A hunter," said Christian. "He probably borrowed the canoe as well." Matty caught the lack of conviction in his voice. "Who knows, he might even bring it back."

He lit the lantern. The log he was sitting on had splintered underneath. When he examined it closely he found the punk wood and earth had been scooped away, the hole filled with pieces of gummy bark.

"That was thoughtful," said Christian, "he left us a pitch deposit!"

"Do you think he's living in Archie's shack?" asked Matty, trying to banish any further thoughts of headhunters. "What will we do if someone's living there?"

"We've got two choices," said Christian. "Either we kick him out and live there like we planned, or we stay here and build another boat. Things could be worse. At least our supplies weren't touched."

But on further investigation Christian found that his tools were missing. His chain saw was gone, too, and his boxes of nails. Matty's pack had been ransacked but nothing had been taken.

"That settles it," said Christian. "We head for the cabin. We may find some tools there – let's hope so. It's a long hike back to civilization."

Christian made a fire with the pitch and splinters; Matty gathered dead limbs and larger pieces of bark. They sat in silence waiting for the flames to die down.

Matty made a pot of coffee which they drank straight from the saucepan sieving out bugs and wood-ash between their teeth. Christian cut a slab off the deer's haunch and cooked it on the end of a stick. Afterwards he doused the fire, covering the embers with dirt.

They turned in for the night. The air was heavy and Matty found sleep impossible. She lit a candle and opened a book. Small insects, attracted by the light, found their way in through a hole in the canvas. Unable to concentrate, she lay awake for hours listening to the forest sounds.

Morning came and there was no sign of the canoe. They sorted their supplies, taking only the perishable items and leaving the rest under the shelter of a root cave. They made an early start.

"Where is the trail?" asked Matty. "I looked yesterday but I couldn't find it."

"It's marked," said Christian. "Archie blazed it. To the right of those rocks and a hundred yards inland. That's where it should begin."

At first the going was difficult. The trail climbed, a tangle of roots, drenched bracken and barbed vines. The salal in places was higher than their heads. Deer had beaten a dark hole through the thick wall of the brush, and the mud was pocked with their tracks. Christian inspected the ground for recent boot marks. To Matty's relief there were none.

They emerged on a ledge where closely packed spruce and hemlock rose to blot out the sky. Moss gripped the bulging roots and dripped from a skirt of branches. An ancient cedar sucked at the earth's core, her tired boughs drooping onto a thick carpet of dry needles. A patch of deer droppings steamed beside the trail.

Their packs snagged on stumps and on low-hanging branches; the path grew steeper, the trees smaller and spindlier. Matty slipped on the moss stumbling over a deadfall. The trail evened out again and they came to a creek, a bright gash through the forest's green darkness.

"Beaver," said Christian, pointing further along the bank. A stand of poplars had been felled across the creek; other trees nearby bore weathered toothmarks where beavers had ringed them six inches deep and then given up the effort. Matty and Christian took off their boots. They waded downstream carefully skirting the deep, swift pools.

On the other side of the creek there was little undergrowth. The path wound along through thickets of alder and birch. Soon the trees gave way to tiny clumps of huckleberry bushes, and they found themselves standing on the edge of the muskeg. They stopped to rest in the waist-high grass.

It had been a long hike from the river, and the sun was low in the sky when they set off again. Stunted pines covered with brightly coloured lichens punctuated the endless tract. They wallowed over the spongy ground through pockets of marsh grass, bog cotton and low-bush cranberry. The mud sloshed and squirted; swamp water oozed over the tops of their boots and Matty had difficulty keeping her balance.

Then, in the middle of nowhere, the trail branched. An old stump stood in the centre of the fork, the four points of the compass engraved on its cut end. An alder stake with a fresh blaze the size of a silver dollar marked the way to the north and when Christian touched the wound the dark blood of the wood came off on his hand.

"Somebody's been here," said Matty.

They took the path that continued to the east. They walked for another hour; the trees grew larger until gradually the muskeg was swallowed by the forest. The trail plunged, following a watercourse; Matty scrambled down the steep slope, slapping at deerflies. Christian startled a doe and her fawn who were grazing beside a clear pool, and Matty, lagging behind, glimpsed a young buck as he slid into a thicket, tree-moss flowing from his antlers.

The silence was broken only by the quick rhythm of their own footsteps. There was a damp chill in the wind. Matty tripped on a root and cried out. The forest felt menacing, full of crouched shadows.

Tracks of hiking boots patterned the mud; she pushed through a clump of skunk cabbage that had already been trampled. Her legs ached. Her feet were clammy and sore. She sat down on a log but the blackflies forced her to keep moving.

Christian was waiting in a patch of light up ahead. She stumbled towards him, flushed and trembling.

The clearing, not a natural one, looked like the aftermath of a tornado. Trees lay shattered in all directions, dropped like a handful of pick-up sticks. Some hung uselessly in the branches of other trees; a gaunt snag groaned under the weight of a dangling hemlock. The ground was littered with debris, the air was filled with the heavy odour of sawdust and crushed needles.

Christian stepped out into the open. A flock of ravens, outraged by the intrusion, took flight calling raucously.

"What's happened?" asked Matty, breathlessly.

"It looks like some kind of logging operation," said Christian.

"The wood's still green. It's been cut recently."

"Within the last week, I'd say."

"What shall we do?" asked Matty.

"We can't go back," said Christian.

They crossed the clear-cut area and picked up the continuation of the trail. The ravens followed, wheeling from tree to tree, circling and diving, talking back and forth. The forest grew darker, the trees thicker. Sometimes their limbs were worn smooth from where, Matty imagined, headhunters had sat waiting for an enemy.

Half a mile later they came to another open space. Here the ground had been levelled, the fallen trees limbed clean and the stumps uprooted and burned. The logs had been split into small, manageable lengths and stacked very neatly to season.

"A woodpile," Matty said, the words catching in her throat. The ravens, having settled into the trees above, had grown abruptly silent.

They proceeded along the path. Within an hour they'd crossed five more logged-off areas, all similar in nature to the second, more organized one.

The forest grew darker and it began to rain. The wet branches clawed at Matty's face. She could hear Christian up ahead, breathing heavily. He stepped on a twig which broke with a loud snap; a bird rose up into the night sky filling the forest with its alarm.

Christian stopped to let her catch up. "We may not find the cabin before dark," he said, "it's further than I remember. I think we've got another hour of twilight. Do you want to keep moving?"

Matty nodded. She felt weak and drained; she longed for sleep. The trail seemed endless to her now, only an act of will kept her body in motion. She felt light-headed, too; tiredness drugged her. Christian pushed ahead through the mottled darkness.

They reached another, larger clearing. This time there were no woodpiles, but what appeared to be a giant kiln shaped like a beaver lodge stood in the middle of their path. One side of the kiln had caved in, exposing a sooty interior of half charcoal and half wood.

Matty slipped off her pack and bent to examine the mound. A signpost partially covered the burnt hole and she read aloud over Christian's shoulder: BEFORE ENLIGHTENMENT, CHOP WOOD AND CARRY WATER. AFTER ENLIGHTENMENT, CHOP WOOD AND CARRY WATER.

"No doubt about it," said Christian. "Someone around here is really enlightened."

The night was closing in on them. Matty unpacked the Trail Mix and they ate together in gloomy silence. She was about to suggest they camp for the night when they heard the sound of a bell.

Browsing among the saplings was a black goat. She was tethered by a chain to a post and had trodden in circles around the post, tangling herself in the process. Christian tried to unravel the chain. The goat started bleating, nibbling at Matty's zipper.

Something moved in the bushes. Something else moaned. The bushes parted and Matty jumped backwards. Two fat chickens flapped into the clearing; the fatter of the two had the other by the throat.

"The welcoming committee," said Christian. The chickens stopped fighting the moment they heard him speak. They fled into the darkness, squawking.

It was pitch dark by the time they reached the final clearing. The rain had stopped and the wind had blown away the clouds. A sickle moon sent a shiver of light through the trees illuminating a cluster of small houses built from cedar poles and shakes, polygonal houses with peaked roofs, facing a central fire-pit. The fire was ablaze and the spicy smell of wood smoke wafted over to where Matty and Christian stood. They heard drumming; guitar music drifted out into the night. A woman was chanting. Children were laughing above the chanting, and a baby was crying.

A figure emerged from one of the doorways, stooped to pick up an axe and began to chop kindling. The shoulders were broad, the arms long and muscular. Matty and Christian stepped into the light.

The woman looked up and put aside the axe. She swept her short-cropped hair out of her strong, open face and walked forward to meet them.

"Welcome," she said: a man's voice. "We've been expecting you."

She shook hands with Christian and embraced Matty.

"My name is Briony," she said. "Welcome to Ephratah."

Part Four
Ephratah

17

"If you take a yellow bird and put a drop of tea extract on its tongue it will fall down dead within fifteen minutes," said Tansy as Matty, huddling over the stove, dropped a handful of tea leaves into a pot of boiling water.

It was their tenth day at Ephratah.

"Any particular reason why the bird has to be yellow?" Christian asked. So far all his questions had been avoided or ignored.

Tansy frowned at him. "Packaged teas contain carcinogenic dyes," she continued, concentrating on Matty, "as well as lethal amounts of caffeine. Tea is a drug. You're poisoning your system."

"I'll have a cup anyway," said Christian, who had ignored all previous attempts to make him change his eating habits. He'd fetched the rest of their supplies from the river despite Briony's warnings about chemically treated foods.

"That's with white granulated sugar," he added.

Tansy looked annoyed. "You shouldn't use industrialized products, it supports the System. Besides, sugar is yin. According to the law of change you must eat yang in a cold climate."

Matty felt she had nothing to contribute. Her purchases from the Food Giant were unfit for human consumption.

Christian poured his own tea and opened a can of tuna.

Tansy left the cabin saying the smell gave her a headache.

Ephratah was a meatless commune. Furthermore, the women had eliminated root vegetables from their diet because "vegetables grown below the ground failed to receive the advantage of direct sunlight on their edible parts." Briony encouraged her women to eat very little. An empty stomach, she proselytized, was a prerequisite for Inner Peace.

In Christian's mind, the very word "peace" was cause for suspicion. He didn't trust Briony. When questioned she denied all knowledge of the canoe; she claimed to know nothing about Christian's missing tools. Supplies were on the way, from where she wouldn't say, and she said she would be able to replace his equipment. Meanwhile he and Matty were welcome to the Guest House.

The Guest House had been prepared for their arrival. The first night Briony brought them fresh bread and soup; Tansy made a salad from edible weeds. A fire crackled in the stove making the room warm and dry. After camping for two weeks Matty was glad of the comfort; she soon stopped thinking about headhunters.

There was little furniture in the room – two bunk beds, a table, two chairs and the stove. Four walls were lined with cedar bark (two were covered with books), the other with newspaper. Part of the latter had been gouged away, and a shrine set up in the alcove.

The shrine, Briony told Matty, had been built in her honour. In the centre, surrounded by seeds, roots, berries, and other offerings, stood a wooden figure carved in the shape of a woman. Cradled between her breasts was a man's head, also made of wood, with pointed ears, large curved horns, and a forked tongue. Between his horns, three women were embracing.

"It symbolizes the ideal society," Briony said, "where the proper study of mankind is woman."

A lamp burned in the window. Above the window was a row of masks, elaborately carved to represent human faces in various stages of pain and ecstasy. All but one–the most recent, Briony explained–had been painted with root dyes and decorated with charcoal. The latest had been painted white.

A cage full of bird skulls hung from the ceiling. A puffball studded with small white feathers revolved on a red string. The cage, Briony said, was the cosmos in miniature; the skulls inside the cage meant freedom through death. The puffball represented the soul in flight; the string, apart from supporting the puffball, had no real importance though the symbolical significances of its colour were various. It was the colour of blood, of fire, of combat, of the passion and sufferings of Christ, of anarchy and danger and the Left wing in politics.

On the table there was an arrangement of dried moss and leaves. There were candle holders made from bones and black candles which, when lit, gave off a strong perfume. Matty blew them out the moment Briony left, and opened the cabin door to let in the fresh air.

The smell lingered. Neither of them felt like eating. Matty sat with her back to the shrine.

"Those masks look real," she said, "especially that recent one."

Something in the expression made her feel uncomfortable. There was sadness in the face, in the high cheekbones, in the black centres of the eyes and the purple cavity of the mouth–an unknown force that filled the room like a heartbeat and seemed to suck her breath away.

They didn't touch their food. Christian prepared for bed and climbed into the lower bunk with *The Compleat Carpenter.* Matty cleared the table and found her way to the outhouse. When she got back, Christian was asleep.

She inspected the bookshelves. She found a text on the art of castrating domestic animals (someone had torn out the illustrations) and a diary containing detailed descriptions of somebody's labour pains. *Beaver Defenders* by Hope Sawyer

Buyukmihci was full of crude marginalia. She curled up in her bunk with a biography of Hitler.

Through a vegetarian diet, she read, Hitler sought to separate himself from the masses. He was also opposed to smoking, drinking, vivisection, and hunting. He often spoke at ladies' luncheons where women applauded his views on vivisection.

There was a photograph of Hitler having breakfast. "It's like eating a corpse," he said, when a waiter brought him a slice of ham. He did, however, provide a choice for his guests. For those who did not observe his vegetarian diet he served sausages made out of his own blood.

Matty fell asleep before the end of the second chapter. When she woke up, hours later, the fire had gone out and the lamp was smoking. She trimmed the wick with Christian's penknife and looked around for more kindling.

The masks seemed to come alive in the flickering lamplight. They leaned towards her, mouths gaping, eyes probing. The white mask carried a strong aura of death. Matty could barely look at it.

She recognized it: the death mask that Dan had worn – the one she'd imagined him wearing – that last day in Old Mystic. In places where the paint was thin she could see the rough wood. The paint on the lips had blistered.

She woke Christian. He moved the lamp away from the window and set it in the alcove. The masks receded into shadow, inhaling their last breath. Christian took Dan off the wall, wrapped him in a towel and pushed him under the bed.

"Take a look at this," he said, squatting next to the paper-lined wall. He read aloud as Matty bent over him, straining her eyes on the small print. *"And the fear of you and the dread of you shall be upon every beast of the earth, and upon every fowl of the air, upon all that moveth upon the earth, and upon all the fishes of the sea; into your hand they are delivered."*

"What is it?" asked Matty. "What does it mean?"

"God said, Behold, I have given you every herb bearing seed,

which is upon the face of all the earth, and every tree in which is the fruit of a tree yielding seed, to you it shall be meat. And to every beast of the earth, and to every fowl of the air, and to every thing that creepeth upon the earth, wherein there is life, I have given green herb for meat."

"What is it?"

"It's the Bible," said Christian. "The whole wall is covered with it. This is the part about the dietary law."

They were, that first night, unaware of the restrictive diet imposed by Briony upon her followers at Ephratah. Puzzled by their strange findings they lit another fire and returned to their beds.

"It's some kind of voodoo," said Matty, shivering.

"Don't worry about it," said Christian. "We aren't going to stay longer than we have to."

Matty opened the biography at Hitler's charcoal landscapes. The fire sizzled and then went out.

She closed the book again. The lamp was still burning in the alcove and she climbed from her bed to extinguish it. Something had been carved above the wooden figure's head: EPHRATAH it said, and, in brackets, BETHLEHEM. A passage from the Bible had been underlined in red.

> *Little children, it is the last time: and as ye have heard that anti-christs shall come, even now there are many anti-christs whereby we know it is the last time.*

"I don't like her," Yarrow snarled, curling her full lips back over her yellow teeth.

"That's the dog imitation I was telling you about," said Tansy. Yarrow was holding forth from her sandbox while Matty stood with Tansy in the doorway to the House of Capricorn. Each of the houses occupied by the women and children at Ephratah represented an astrological sign. Tansy, who lived with Yarrow, had invited Matty to tea.

"I don't *want* her to stay," Yarrow pouted, attacking the sand with a plastic hatchet. "When is she going? When is she!"

"Ignore her," Tansy said to Matty. "She's just testing you. Isn't the sandbox great? Rasputin packed the sand all the way from the river!"

"Rasputin?" asked Matty, as Yarrow hurled herself onto the ground, screwing her fists into her eyes.

"It's a horrible sandbox and you're not allowed in!" she cried.

"Yarrow!" exclaimed Tansy, helplessly. "You must learn to share your things! You don't want Matty to think you're a selfish girl, do you?"

"I don't care. It's mine mine mine mine mine mine mine mine," Yarrow wailed, lunging with both feet until most of the sand lay scattered outside the box.

"Lucky you, owning such a big sandbox," said Matty, hoping to discourage further acts of violence.

"I'm not lucky," Yarrow raged. "*You're* the lucky!"

"That's right. I'm lucky too!"

"No, you're not. You're not not not not not not not not not not. You're a stupid pooh, that's what!"

"She's too much, isn't she?" Tansy said, shaking her head in bewilderment. "Kids are so *open* these days!"

"What sign is she?" Yarrow demanded, looking at Matty and gouging from her bulbous nose a juicy chunk of snot.

"Freud says it's quite natural," Tansy hastened, seeing Matty's disgust. "Yarrow may be a nuisance sometimes, but you can't say she's inhibited!"

"What *sign* are you?" sniffed the child, satisfied that she was the centre of attention.

"Capricorn," said Matty quietly, wishing she were anything else. Yarrow was the embodiment of all that sign's negative aspects.

"No you're not," Yarrow defied. "You're a pooh-pum. Pee-po-pooh!"

Tansy sighed. "I'll sure be glad when she's over this lavatorial stage," she said under her breath. "I don't know where she gets it from. I suppose it means she's healthy though."

She turned to speak directly to Yarrow. "You're being difficult. Matty *is* a Capricorn. She was born the day after you were, on the fifteenth of January."

"How come she's so old, then? Why is she?"

"She was born *before* you were, that's why. Years before. I feel you're being hostile, Yarrow. Do you want to talk about it?"

"What's her *real* name," Yarrow shouted. "Her real real real real real real name?"

Tansy motioned Matty inside. "She's jealous of you, I think. We better leave her alone for a while."

Matty followed.

"No one is allowed in my sandbox and I'm staying right here you stupid poohs!"

Tansy closed the door apologetically.

"She'll get used to you. Yarrow's pretty up-front about her emotions. You have to be firm with her at first. That way she'll learn to respect you."

"I've never had to deal with children," said Matty, grimly, "and I don't know if I've got the patience. What did she mean by asking about my *real* name? Do you think she'd rather call me Martha?"

Tansy laughed. "You've probably noticed by now but we all use organic names here–mostly the names of herbs and flowers. Betony reads charts. You'll like her, she's a Sagittarius. She knows what planets rule which plants. If you know your sun sign and your rising sign she can calculate the rest. You'll need a new name, at least while you're with us. We want you to feel at home."

Matty said she didn't want to change her name. She felt her own was quite suitable; she felt it belonged to her.

Tansy shook her head. "We don't belong to ourselves in

any respect," she said. "We belong first to the Chela and secondly to Briony as the Chela's representative."

"What's the Chela?" Matty asked.

Tansy looked terrified. She glanced around the room, leaned close to Matty's ear, and said in a hushed voice, "I wasn't supposed to tell you. He hears everything."

She handed Matty a cup of clear liquid with a twig floating on the top.

"Mu tea," she said. "It's made from sixteen different plants. It's good for your bladder or your heart, I forget which. Valerian's the expert on herbal remedies."

"I've got a tall thin stranger," said Matty, fishing out the twig.

"That'll be Rasputin. Sometimes he comes with messages from the Chela." She stopped, her face twisting from some obvious source of unhappiness. "I had, we had a sort of a thing happening once."

"Who's Rasputin? Is he Yarrow's father?"

"Of course not," Tansy said. "There's only one Real Father. It's the Chela. He only has to *breathe* and you'll conceive. Celandine, that's Yarrow's mother, she has a baby every year. She's due to deliver any day now."

"I thought Yarrow was *yours*," said Matty, bewildered.

Tansy shook her head again. "No way, but she's a Capricorn like me. Celandine is a Leo. She couldn't have a Capricorn in the House of Leo but she's got Thistle's child instead. Thistle's Peony is a Leo. See how it works?"

Matty nodded, dubiously. "What about you? Have you had any babies?"

"I had twins. I lost them. Briony still blames Rasputin. She thinks I had twins because Rasputin's a schizophrenic and I slept with him."

"Did you?" asked Matty.

"We slept together, but I didn't *sleep* with him," said Tansy. "Know what I mean? I couldn't be unfaithful to the

Chela even if I tried. The Chela is everywhere. He's part of me."

Matty caught herself following Tansy's gaze. "What does he look like?" she asked.

Tansy shrugged. "I've never seen him. Briony says he's not a man or a woman. He's a Glorious Power.

"I know he wants a son more than anything," she continued, "and so far only his daughters have lived. Once a month we have a Pregnancy Wishes Ritual where we ask God to send us a new Messiah. One of us will be chosen to be his earthly mother."

The Chela came down from the charcoal burners' camp, a self-sufficient commune some ten miles north of Ephratah, to attend each Pregnancy Wishes Ritual. His goal was to release mankind from the hold of Satan, and to win the world over for the new, as yet unborn, Messiah. When he wasn't participating in the Ritual, or soul-travelling in other parts of the country, the Chela was out with his men making charcoal.

"You saw those clearings on your way in from the river? And the giant kiln? That's their work."

Matty asked why they were making charcoal.

"We need charcoal to make gunpowder. When the Messiah comes there'll be a world where there's no more crime or poverty."

Matty took a swig of her tea wishing it were something stronger.

"Yin people should drink this every day," said Tansy. "It's a very yang beverage."

18

"This is you," said Briony, marking their cabin with a red X. Christian sat in the doorway eating the last of the curried venison. Matty, in deference to Briony, had gone without breakfast.

Briony had spread out a diagram of the commune. It was circular in outline with the outer border concentrated around a fixed point, the Guest House.

"It's a mandala," she said. "It circumscribes the territory we operate in."

"Get many guests?" asked Christian, scraping the sides of the dish with his spoon.

"Some," said Briony.

"How do you do it, starve them to death?"

Briony looked at him, unsmiling. "Nobody needs meat," she said. "Besides, vegetarians are stronger. They have more endurance." She cited examples: the elephant that could outrun the lion; the plant-eating Japanese wrestlers who were among the strongest men in the world; she herself who could move heavy furniture alone. Meat-eating, she said, was imitative, like drinking and smoking; people would eat less meat if offered a greater variety of vegetables. A child, she argued, would never choose meat if given a choice between meat, fruit or candy.

Hitler thought that vegetarians did not sweat as offensively as meat-eaters, Matty added. He thought underwear stains were increased by the consumption of flesh foods.

"Hitler was right," agreed Briony. "A meat-eater is quite different from a vegetable eater. He is aggressive while the vegetarian lives in the diurnal tranquillity of a flower, opening to light, then closing with the day's end."

"Amen," said Christian.

"Tell us about the mandala," said Matty, trying to manoeuvre the conversation to more neutral ground.

The word "mandala" was Sanskrit meaning circle, Briony said. It must be drawn correctly and with the right vitality so as to connect it with the unseen world. It was not a matter to be undertaken lightly.

Christian sat down on the other side of the table. He was about to interrupt when Matty kicked him.

Briony was explaining the components of the mandala. The inner compound, consisting of the twelve cabins surrounding the Guest House, was shaped like a pentagon. The pentagon was contained within a square and at each corner of the square there was a building: Communal Hall, Meditation Hut, Food Barn, and the Manger.

The mandala, Briony said, was also used to draw down and house the spirits. By means of spells, offerings, and invocations, the practitioner could summon spiritual beings to occupy a place assigned to them in the diagram, and charge it with their presence. It was then called a *yantra*, or an engine of power. Every yantra differed according to the power of the occupying entities.

"The Manger, for instance. The yantra there is sexual. It represents the generative female organs."

"That explains it," said Christian, sarcastically. "That accounts for the overflowing of unrestrained lust around here."

Christian had found the women cold and unattractive.

He'd complained to Matty that they looked like men, that he couldn't tell one from the other.

Tansy had told Matty the women looked that way on purpose. They cut their hair short so they could do the same work as men. They wore loose-fitting clothes so they could move about freely in the bush.

"Does the Guest House have a yantra?" asked Matty. She took Christian's hand under the table, and squeezed it.

"It's mystical," Briony said. "It's all things past and future. This is a place of resolution. The masks say everything."

Matty apologized for removing the death mask from the wall. She hoped it hadn't offended the occupying deity, but the mask had frightened her.

"Some yantras take on a life of their own," said Briony, "and they can have a very destructive power. But sometimes it's just phantom shapes emanating from our own minds. Partial reflections of our inner natures."

"I hate to interrupt the flow," said Christian, "but would anyone like a cup of coffee?"

Matty shook her head. Briony told him she didn't use drugs. She smoothed the mandala as if it had suddenly developed wrinkles. Matty gave Christian a look of annoyance and he went outside with his coffee.

"We've developed about ten acres," said Briony. "There's a vegetable garden and a swimming hole. That's the path to the spring where we get our drinking water." She indicated a dotted line to the north and west. "Beyond that there's the lake. It forms our northern boundary. Everything inside the circle is ours. The rest belongs to the charcoal burners."

Matty had told Christian about the charcoal burners. Tansy had been severely reprimanded for revealing their existence, and Briony did not respond to further questioning by Christian. She told him she had asked for the supplies he wanted. He could speak to them personally about getting a boat.

Briony rolled up the mandala and tucked it into her pocket. Matty followed her out into the sunshine.

Christian was sitting in silence on the steps of the outhouse.

"Briony's offered to show us around," said Matty.

He belched and looked up at Briony. "I beg your pardon," he said, "It must have been that curry. I suppose you're going to tell me that I haven't been eating yin."

"On the contrary," said Briony, smugly. "Heartburn is caused by excessive acidity. You need to yangize more. You're not following the law of change. You must modify your diet to fit with time and place."

Matty was beginning to tire of Christian's cynical remarks. "We're getting a guided tour," she said. "The walk will do you good."

"I don't need healing," he said, impatiently, "I need a drink. You two go ahead on your own. I'll catch up to you later."

"Is he always so defensive?" asked Briony, as they started up the trail that led to the Communal Hall.

"Only lately," said Matty, "ever since the canoe disappeared."

The Communal Hall was located in the northwest corner of the square, as indicated by the mandala. Briony walked ahead.

The trail was well used. In places where water had collected in dark pools they had to climb up over mossy windfalls and beat a new path through clumps of tangled bracken. A solitary raven barked from a tall cedar, startling Matty.

They had come to a clearing. A geodesic dome, covered with black plastic, rose from the ground before them. The dome had been designed to be invisible from the air, the plastic held in place by fishnet, spruce boughs, and stones. Their next project, Briony said, was to erect an Outdoor Dwelling. With complete grounds enclosed by a dome, eliminating rain, wind, snow, and insects, houses themselves would eventually be unnecessary.

Briony took Matty's hand. "We come here for group

awareness," she said, leading Matty into the clearing. "The dome shape is conducive."

Weekly Un-Meatings were held in the Communal Hall as well. The women gathered for a meal, discussed problems, exchanged ideas, and played music. The children received instruction on various arts and crafts. There were Prayer Breakfasts on Thursdays, and Pregnancy Wishes Rituals once a month.

Matty stepped over a steep board guarding the threshold. Ostensibly the board was a protection against floods, but Briony said its true purpose was to repel demons. There were no windows in the structure because windows "obstructed vision." Eyeglasses were not allowed at Ephratah for the same reason, and there were no mirrors.

They went inside. Briony struck a match and lit the lamps. WOMEN, ARE YOU *STILL* HUMAN CHAUVINISTS? THE ALL-COMPASSIONATE FEMINIST IS A VEGETARIAN, read a large notice over the sink. A bowl of fermenting soy beans lay on the counter.

"They'll be ready to eat in a couple of months," said Briony, indicating the beans. She pushed aside a curtain that covered the space beneath the counter, and brought out an earthenware jar. "Valerian's experimenting," she said. "It's a cure for ageing."

Matty surveyed the room. A sturdy wooden table took up most of the space; there were two rows of cold, hard benches. At the head of the table there was a pulpit and beyond that an altar. The headless body of Christ, crucified, swung on a meat hook from the ceiling.

"The Chela carried him all the way from Toronto," said Briony.

She led Matty to the altar and picked up two buckets, one containing septic-smelling mud and the other solid wax.

"The kids were creating candles last week," she explained, setting the buckets aside. "We also gave them a lesson in the healing properties of mud."

Matty nodded, her eyes fastened on the headless crucifix.

"Termites," said Briony. "The head was completely eaten. The rest of the body's infested, look!" She pointed to the exit holes in the belly. "Those have been made by emerging adults."

The dangling saviour had also been used as a dartboard. His heart, a luminous red bulge, was the target and Briony pulled a yellow dart from his left armpit.

"That was Yarrow's idea," said Briony. "She was expressing her contempt for the gigantic Catholic cosmos."

"How many other children are there?" asked Matty, turning her back on the cadaver.

"Seven," replied Briony. "And there are sixteen women. Altogether there are twenty-four of us. With you – and Christian – that makes twenty-five."

"I see I've been elevated," said Christian, tripping over the board at the door, "from *persona non grata*, to *non persona*. I'd like to know what's happening here. Our supply of whisky is missing."

Briony said she knew nothing about it. "You're quick to accuse," she said. "You've probably misplaced it somewhere in your cabin."

"There were six full bottles," he said, "at the bottom of my pack. Unlike the canoe they couldn't get up and walk."

Briony replaced the board over the threshold. Her manner seemed to convey that all would be explained to them in due course. Christian could see there was no use in pursuing the matter. He went outside and waited for Matty to join him.

"Was anything else taken?" she asked, when Briony stayed behind to close up the hall.

Christian shook his head. "My gun's hidden," he said. "They won't find the ammunition, either. Seems like we're being treated like more than just guests. I think we should leave while we've still got the chance."

Briony approached them, smiling cheerfully. "Don't go yet," she said, "you haven't seen anything. I want you to see the square, at least. As an integrated whole, not an assortment of parts."

The Meditation Hut lay in the northeast corner of the square; they reached it by a trail leading due east from the Communal Hall. Christian said he was feeling everything *but* transcendental. He stayed outside whistling while the women looked around.

"Whistling discharges yin," said Briony. "It's a normal reaction, like sneezing, coughing and hiccupping. Christian is deficient in Vitamin B. Suspiciousness and skepticism, they're always the first symptoms."

Continuing to the south they reached the Food Barn. A variety of grains, vegetables, dried fruits, herbs, and spices were stored inside waterproof barrels under the floor. Briony said there was enough food to last a lifetime.

Visitors were not allowed in the Manger. A retreat for the women after their Pregnancy Wishes Ritual, it was situated in the southwest corner of the square. The other outbuildings included a potting shed, a woodworking shop, a stable for the goat, and a chicken house. The chickens, who had been raised as pets, had abandoned their shelter. They were free spirits, Briony said, roosting in the trees at night. All but two had been dragged off by raccoons.

Avoiding the Manger, they made a complete circle of the square, finishing in the west by the vegetable garden. The garden was not doing well due to the late spring and heavy rainfall, Briony said. There were maggoty radishes and a few unhappy cabbages. A clump of parsley that had survived the winter was gradually being choked out by an edible weed transplanted from the lakeside. A high wooden fence surrounded the garden but even so, Briony complained, something had managed to eat all the lettuce.

"Our soil is rich," she said, "because we recycle our shit. Compost it for a year or so and it's the best fertilizer you can get." Before Christian had time to question the nutritive value of vegetarian excrement, Briony had moved on to the swimming hole.

"It freezes during the winter," she said, "so most of us wash at home. If you're feeling healthy you can chop a hole in the ice, but it starts to freeze over again almost immediately. We have to pack our drinking water. If you walk to the spring in the early evening there's a good chance you'll see deer – sometimes a bear and quite often beaver. As long as you're relaxed they won't run from you. Stand still and breathe deeply from the area of the intestines. Breathing is essential," she said, staring intently at Christian.

"You're not going to cut anything with *that*!" Tansy gasped, her face a mask of horror. "That's a butcher's knife. Can't you feel the vibes? You'll have to throw those onions out. They can go on the compost, but don't tell Briony. She'd *murder* me. I've caused enough problems already."

"Sorry," said Matty, "I wasn't thinking. The knife was clean, though. It's been washed since the last time Christian used it."

"That doesn't make any difference," said Tansy. "The point is it's been used to cut flesh. You have to boil it to get rid of all the cells. You have to purify your body by not eating meat. It takes *seven years* for your cells to replace themselves. I've got two months to go and I'll be a pure vegetarian."

Matty sheathed the knife. "I'm really very sorry. I didn't know what I was doing."

Tansy sighed. "There's so *much* to know," she said. "Some things look harmless when they're actually deadly. We all grew up eating eggs, right? We might as well have been eating arsenic!"

"Eggs?" asked Matty.

"Pure poison," said Tansy.

That afternoon Tansy took Matty to see Betony. The house

of Sagittarius was similar in appearance to the House of Capricorn only the ceiling was covered with diagrams of the heavens and there was no skylight. Valerian made a tea distilled from cornflower petals, saying that it was a good remedy for snakebite and that the juice of the seeds could be used to treat the plague.

"Valerian's a genius," said Tansy.

Betony was examining Matty's birth chart. "Four o'clock in the afternoon, the fifteenth of January, 1954. That's when you were born?"

"I think so," said Matty, lowering her voice to the same level of intensity. When Betony spoke, her upper lip quivered, forcing the observer into sympathetic twitching bouts. Her eyes were unfocused, a pale liquid green.

"This is a serious matter," said Betony. "I assumed you were born at that time and I've drawn up your chart accordingly. If you got the time wrong, none of this will make any sense."

Betony moved closer. Matty experienced a muscle spasm in her right leg.

"You need henbane, or saxifrage and henbane together," Betony diagnosed as Matty massaged the cramp. "Valerian will make you an infusion."

"It may be a simple calcium deficiency," said Tansy. "People born under our sign often have trouble with their joints."

Betony handed Matty her chart with its numerous signs and symbols. "It looks complicated," she said, "unless you know something about astrology."

Matty confessed that she knew very little. She had read her horoscope in the daily *Oracle* until she'd discovered it was written by a computer.

Betony summed up the two types of Capricornians by describing the two types of goats: the giddy mountain goat, stepping neatly from crag to crag, always moving on to nibble the greener grass further up the mountain; and the domestic goat restricted to the small patch of grass within the circle allowed her by a post and chain. "You want to break free," she said, "but the mountain overwhelms you. Your chain means security. You lack confidence, you're too conventional."

"You should take up rock-climbing," Tansy interrupted. "It's good for your joints."

Betony agreed. "Saturn is your ruling planet," she said, "and it is associated with the bones. Also with inevitable slow change and inhibition. Inhibition cramps the whole personality and takes a long time to control."

"We can help you," said Tansy.

"You've got a lot to work on," said Betony, "but you have good endurance and self-discipline. In the past there is a difficult father and a domineering mother. There may have been psychological deprivation as a child and as a result you have too much imagination.

"You were married once – unsuccessfully. No children of your own. There is some suggestion of infertility. Sexual inhibition as well.

"In the future I see serious probings into death and the after-life. Something unhealthy – perhaps an illness? At some point a great sacrifice. But it's not very clear."

"What about a name?" asked Tansy. "What plants does she have to choose from?"

Betony consulted a battered herbal. "Let's see, she could be a Hemlock or a Bracken. Amaranth or Indigo."

"Amaranth," said Valerian, "that suits her."

"Of the genus *Amaranthus*, which includes Love-Lies-Bleeding," said Betony. "It's an imaginary flower that lives forever."

19

"It's raining again," said Christian.

Matty lay on her bunk counting the drops of condensation that trickled down the skylight.

"Rain is a source of life," said Tansy. "It's nature's semen."

Matty closed her eyes. She pictured a giant penis in the sky, ejaculating. Valerian had made her a potion for her joints. The drink made her drowsy and she'd returned to her bed complaining of dizziness.

"You're just experiencing the Twilight Sleep," said Tansy. "Henbane has a sedative effect."

"I warned you not to take it," said Christian, forcing Matty to drink copious amounts of black coffee. "Henbane's a deadly poison."

"It's a herb of Saturn," said Tansy. "It's perfectly harmless. Besides, Valerian mixed it with nettle seed. Nettles destroy the toxic principle."

Another week had passed and the supplies Christian needed had still not arrived. Concerned about Matty, about their mutual well-being, Christian decided to go in search of the charcoal burners' camp.

"I found a kind of track," he said. "It runs along the lake. If it doesn't lead anywhere I'll try that trail over the muskeg.

The trail we didn't take, remember? The one that branched to the north."

Matty nodded, sleepily. She remembered, from an immeasurably distant past, their journey in from the river and the stump they'd found with the strange markings. Christian wanted her to go with him now, but she didn't have the strength to go anywhere.

"I'll be back," he said. "If I don't find help soon we'll just have to hike our way out of here."

Briony tried to discourage him. "If you're determined to go," she said, "I can't stop you. But you're wasting your time, I'm warning you."

Christian went anyway. Briony walked with him as far as the Communal Hall. She returned, an hour later, with Valerian.

Matty, at Tansy's suggestion, had moved to Christian's bed. Her dizziness had increased, and Tansy was afraid she might roll out of the top bunk and land on the floor.

Nothing felt stranger to Matty than her own body. She felt removed from the world around her, which in itself seemed vaguely insubstantial. She could feel the slight pressure of a thumb on her wrist. Briony was taking her pulse.

Tansy lit a stick of incense. She bolted the door and covered the window with sacking. Valerian dusted the shrine as though she were rehearsing a familiar scene in which Matty's role had long ago been decided.

The room smelled of jasmine, of musk and cinnamon. The women spoke to each other in what sounded to Matty like another language. She closed her eyes again, lulled by the dusky voices.

The only light came down through the ceiling. The rain had stopped and the sun shone like a spotlight on the centre of the cabin floor. Tansy unfolded a bamboo mat and laid it in the sunbeam. In the middle of the mat she placed a small shaving mirror.

Matty had not seen a mirror since arriving at Ephratah – hers had been confiscated. Her face must have registered surprise because Briony nodded, smiling.

"Clarity comes with the giving up of self," she said. "When you stop attributing selfhood to mirror images, then you have gained control over your body."

Tansy pointed at the mirror. "This is a mirror," she said, as if Matty were incapable of seeing for herself. "Do you recognize it?"

Matty shook her head. It was a perfectly ordinary shaving mirror; there was nothing special about it.

"It belonged to a man," said Valerian. "Tansy knew him."

"I defied the Chela," said Tansy. "I looked in the mirror."

"She saw her reflection," said Briony to Matty, "and now she can't find herself."

"She's separated from her soul," said Valerian.

Matty stared at the women blankly. Valerian said the man was a devil. He'd arrived at Ephratah shortly before Matty and Christian and he'd caused Tansy to sin against the Chela.

The man had taken ill suddenly. He had died in his sleep, in the same bed on which Matty was now lying. His ghost had snatched the soul of the last person reflected in the glass, and that person had been Tansy.

"You are going to help," Briony said, taking Matty's wrist again. "Tansy will be trying to exorcise his spirit."

"If the mirror breaks," said Valerian, "he will leave her body. His soul will take possession of your soul, instead."

Matty suddenly realized – it was Dan's mirror. She remembered laughing at him for carrying it everywhere. Apart from the moustache, which he trimmed frequently, his face had never grown any hair.

She tried to speak but her mouth wasn't working.

"The incense has made her sleepy," said Briony.

"She's still experiencing the Twilight Sleep," said Tansy. "I think we should give her the rest of that potion."

Briony lifted Matty's head while Valerian opened her

mouth and Tansy forced her to drink. Matty felt an invisible current passing through her as if her body were an instrument playing up and down the scales. The room seemed to reverberate with sound though she couldn't tell where the sounds were coming from. The room was swallowing her like a vast human throat.

Her body became liquid; her ears filled up with the sound of waves breaking. For a moment she couldn't see anything. A sea-wall of darkness drowned the light.

"As waves come with water and flames with fire, so the universe waves with us," said Tansy, reciting the ancient Tantric scripture. Matty felt the wave engulfing her, sucking her inside out. Her body became a dance of fragments, her mind a centre of gravity welding the fragments together.

She lay with her eyes wide open. Her body, on the outside, was completely paralyzed; on the inside she was dancing down a hallway of mirrors. In every mirror she saw her face reflected, her self-image clarified in the infinite regressions. Her face became all ages at once – her old woman's skull had the same form as a newborn child's. The process of aging became clear in all its aspects, in the falling away of flesh, in the revelation of bone.

"I think she's asleep," she heard Valerian saying. "She won't remember any of this. I put something in the potion that will help her forget everything."

Again Matty felt Briony's hand on her pulse. "Her pulse is weaker," Briony said, "she hasn't much strength. Her soul must have left her. I think we can start."

Valerian and Tansy carried her from the bed. They strapped her into a chair where she was forced to sit upright, facing the shrine. The alcove was now lit up with candles.

Briony pulled the death mask out from under the bed. She undid Matty's shirt. Then she stood the mask in Matty's lap, cradling it between her breasts.

In Matty's state every movement was exaggerated. She watched Tansy undress; the removal of the sweater was like the painful removal of a bandage, the skin peeling away and the flesh healing all in the same motion.

Beneath her baggy clothes, Tansy had a girl's body. Her breasts were small with large nipples that tilted slightly upwards. She had no pubic hair – whether it had never grown or had been shaved recently, Matty couldn't tell. Perhaps Dan had made her shave, squatting over his shaving mirror. He'd made Matty do that once, but he'd not been happy when the hair grew back coarse and prickly.

Valerian moved the mirror to one side and covered it with a cloth. Tansy lay down on her back, spreading her legs so Briony could kneel between them. Using a soft brush made from human hair, Briony began to paint Tansy's body with bright red pigment.

She circled the breasts, dabbing at the nipples with the tip of her brush. Tansy didn't move. Her breasts seemed to shrink as her nipples hardened.

Briony worked down over the surface of Tansy's belly using her bellybutton as a paint pot. She dipped the brush in as deep as it would go, jiggling it from side to side. The expression on Tansy's face didn't change though Matty thought she caught a flicker of agitation.

Briony stood back looking satisfied. She made a frame with her fingers, considering Tansy from all angles as if she were a canvas.

Tansy raised her buttocks, spreading her legs wider. Briony knelt again, stroking the soft flesh that enclosed the clitoris. She brushed the vulva lips, up and down, gently, flitting backwards and forwards over the tip of the clitoris until it was swollen.

Valerian bent down and kissed Tansy's nipples. "Open yourself," she whispered. "You're resisting the flow. Make yourself open. Try to touch your soul."

She kissed Tansy on the mouth, moistening it with the tip of her tongue. Tansy arched her body, and pushed. The lips of her vulva parted.

Briony rolled Tansy over onto her stomach. Valerian blindfolded her and set the mirror in position. Tansy was made to straddle the glass so that her genitals were perfectly reflected. Briony annointed her back with the pigment.

"Can you feel anything yet?" she asked Tansy. "Have you found your soul?"

Tansy shook her head.

"Then open yourself more. Go to the centre. Find your soul and purify it."

Briony took Tansy's right hand and guided it between her legs. The delicate pressure of the brush had made her wet; she slipped a finger between her open lips and began stroking. Her fingers worked quickly as Briony and Valerian stood over her.

"Go to the centre of yourself," said Briony. "Find yourself and open out."

Tansy pinched her lips together, then continued stroking herself until the lips had opened again. She stuck her forefinger into her vagina and pulled it out, wet. Moistening her asshole, she circled it with her little finger.

"Exorcise your shame," said Briony. Tansy stuck her little finger up into her asshole.

The fingers made a little clicking sound as Tansy rocked backwards and forwards over the mirror. The whole area of her sex was shining wet between her legs. The rhythm of her fingers became the rhythm of Matty's heartbeat. Her breath echoed that beat; she felt a tremor from the earth's core rattling her skull.

"Slow down," Valerian said to Tansy. "Take your time. Coax him–coax him out of you."

Briony pulled Tansy's hand away from her sex. She handed Valerian a whip of plaited leather.

"Cool her off a bit," said Briony. "Do it however you like, but keep it in mind–she slept with a man!"

Valerian flicked the whip between Tansy's legs, slowly, until the ends of the leather were wet. She made Tansy spread her buttocks with one hand, until her asshole was fully exposed. Then she lifted the whip and let it fall across the opening. Tansy did not move and Valerian struck again, leaving a red mark.

"Strike harder," said Briony. "Exorcise the burning."

Tansy tensed her muscles, awaiting the blows. Each time the whip cracked, Matty flinched. In the hallway of mirrors she could hear glass breaking.

Valerian was striking harder and harder. Blood-streaked weals appeared along Tansy's back. With each stroke of the whip her body contracted. Finally she collapsed, sobbing, on top of the shaving mirror.

One knee hit the glass and the glass shattered. Briony pushed Tansy to one side. She held the broken mirror up to Matty's face, repeating a magic formula, guaranteed, she told Valerian, to "penetrate the dense barrier of the material sphere" and relocate Dan's soul somewhere inside Matty. Matty did not recognize her face in the cracked mirror. Her flesh was dissolving. Pieces of herself came away in her hands.

Tansy lay on the floor, moaning. Briony and Valerian bent down and embraced her. Valerian blew out the candles and removed the carved figure from the shrine. Briony took the death mask and put it in a box.

Matty understood, finally, why the shrine had been built in her honour. It was Dan's head she had been holding in her lap, an image of Dan's selfhood. He must have arrived at Ephratah shortly before she and Christian had.

He took ill suddenly. That was not like Dan.

Matty felt ill herself. Valerian unstrapped her from the chair. She slumped forward and down, her head lolling. They carried her to the bed, the same bed in which Dan had died.

He died in his sleep. It wasn't possible.

Briony sat down laying a cool hand on Matty's shoulder. Gently she began to massage her neck muscles.

Matty wanted to sleep. She had lost contact with her body.

"She's stopped breathing," said Briony. "She's transcended the physical."

"You stopped breathing," said Christian. "You nearly died. Lucky for you I got back when I did."

"Was I sick?" Matty asked.

"You mean you don't remember?"

"She doesn't *mean* anything," said Briony, sharply. "You're trying to confuse her. She wasn't going to die, whatever you think. She was soul-travelling."

Briony was sitting at the table with Valerian. On the floor at their feet was an old steel trap and, lying stiff on the bamboo mat, a dead beaver.

"They had good reasons for not wanting us to visit the Manger," said Christian. "Just as I suspected–it's Archie's old shack. They've turned it into a tanning shed. They're trappers!"

Christian had followed the track around the lake. There he'd discovered the trapped beaver. Later, in the back room of the Manger, in a vault under the floor where Archie had kept his supplies, he'd found more than a dozen tanned hides.

He picked up the trap and carried it over to Matty. One time she'd gone with Dan to set traps out on the claim. Beavers had blocked one of the major salmon streams, downing stands of commercial timber and flooding the surrounding area. The company had tried dynamiting the dams, but the beaver always rebuilt in the same location.

Christian set the trap down beside her. It was the same kind of trap Dan had used, with a chain attached by a swivel to prevent kinking. They'd waded out into the water to cover up their tracks, and fastened the chain to a stake that had been driven into the creekbed. Dan baited a twig and left it sticking out of the water a few inches above the trap. When the beaver smelled the musk he would step on the trap and spring it.

Matty looked into the snapped jaws, imagining the caught beaver. When he dived down to try to hide in the deep water, the chain would prevent him going very far.

"The beaver doesn't suffer," said Briony. "He drowns instantly."

"Beavers need thinning," said Valerian, "or else they would die naturally."

"With that kind of logic," said Christian, "you could rationalize killing one another."

Briony frowned. "We're part of a complex eco-system," she said. "We provide the beaver with a challenge. They're surviving better than ever. The population has tripled since we arrived."

"We're not like people who go out and kill for pleasure," said Valerian. "We feel a far greater emotional attachment to the animals we kill than the average person feels for the cow when he eats a hamburger. We don't waste any part of the animal, either. Even the testicles have a purpose: we use them as fertilizer."

It was once believed, Valerian said, that castoreum, an oily secretion used in medicine and perfumery, was situated in the testicles. According to a fable, the beaver castrated itself when pursued by a hunter. Since the hunter wanted it only for its testicles, the animal then escaped. Should another hunter pursue it, it showed its incompleteness and was left unmolested. "The beaver is a saint," said Valerian. "He triumphs over the lust of the flesh."

"The Chela says we should behave like the beaver," said Briony. "We should sever ourselves from our sins and throw them in the face of the Devil."

"Christ," said Christian.

Matty looked at the dead beaver. She looked at Briony and Valerian. "What do you do with the meat?" she asked.

"You're trivializing death," said Briony, "with questions like that. You deprive death of its dignity by worrying about the remains."

"The Chela blesses the body," added Valerian. "He says that the animal understands in its soul what its purpose on earth was meant to be. He says it has offered itself to support our cause."

"Oh," said Christian, "what cause is that? The cause of the all-compassionate feminist?"

"You don't understand," said Briony. "Death is something we earn; it's not a given right. No one dies until he deserves to. It's an honour bestowed on those who have lived."

"Who makes these decisions?" said Christian. "Who decides if I deserve to die?"

Briony looked at him coldly. "The Chela decides," she said.

20

The Chela was ready to receive Christian. Briony said he'd sent word from his camp, and she drew Christian a map of how to get there. Christian had set off immediately.

When he'd been gone for over a week, Matty came down with a cold. Rather than face another grim day alone in the Guest House, she moved into the House of Capricorn. Tansy had offered to take care of her. She administered Valerian's potions and massaged Matty's chest with Tiger Balm.

Matty had the bed under the window. She was dozing: Valerian had given her something to help her sleep. Tansy had gone to an Un-Meating and had stayed out later than she'd intended.

The floorboards creaked as Yarrow tossed in her crib. The crib had been bolted to the floor: as a baby Yarrow had forcefully moved it about the room, beating her head against the bars until the wood broke.

Matty shifted, coughing. Someone was standing at the head of her bed. He reached down and covered her mouth with his hand. Her eyes, wide open, stared blindly into the dark. The hand pressed harder, preventing an outcry.

"Shhh," he whispered. "Get up. I have to talk to you."

The pressure of his hand softened. Matty took a deep breath and pushed him away.

"Shhh. We haven't much time. You've got to come with me. Don't wake anyone."

"There's only Yarrow," said Matty. "She'll sleep through anything. Tell me what's the matter."

She reached down beside the bed and lit a candle. "Tansy's over at the Communal Hall. Chris, what happened?"

Christian slumped into a chair. His clothes were in shreds, his face was battered and swollen. His head had been shaved and in the middle of his forehead was the sign of the cross. It had been neatly cut with a razor blade and the wound packed with charcoal to leave a permanent mark.

"I refused to join their religion," he said. "I think they took it personally." He managed a grin, though his mouth was crooked. "Too bad my father can't see me now. Another Boy For Jesus!"

Christian hadn't eaten since he left Ephratah. He hadn't been allowed to sleep. He'd been interrogated for hours at a time. When he wouldn't renounce the world he was stripped and beaten. He'd been tied to a stake in a circle of burning charcoal. He'd been taken out into the forest where he'd been shot at by men with painted bodies, men wearing masks similar to the ones hanging in the Guest House.

"Who were they?" Matty asked. She couldn't look at him. His face looked worse than any mask she'd seen.

He pulled back the covers and took Matty's hands. There was a tightness about his lips, as though he were trying to keep some kind of secret to himself, one that was too painful to inflict upon anyone.

"They're . . . it's some kind of . . . they had no intention of letting us leave. They took our boat, they took our supplies. We'll have to make a run for it. Get your clothes on, quickly!"

"I'm sick," said Matty. "I can't go."

"You've got two choices," said Christian. "Either you get moving or . . . there's no question. We've got to make a run for it."

"Or what?" said Matty.

Christian didn't answer.

Matty lay down. She felt the sickness coming, her body being seized by a nightmare of awareness. She lay face down, trembling. Christian gripped her shoulder and began shaking her.

"Nothing's going to happen," he said. "Not if you get up. You must. They'll be looking for us."

Christian had escaped while the men were eating supper. They'd left him unguarded because he was too weak to go anywhere. During the whole ordeal he had not met the Chela. The Chela was soul-travelling in northern Saskatchewan.

Matty stood up. She was too weak to care about anything but sleep. She tried to concentrate on what Christian was saying. It was important to listen, if she wanted to live.

He took her in his arms. Always before they had avoided touching, as if touching might destroy the closeness between them. Now she felt closer to Christian than ever. His body felt familiar, a part of herself.

He stroked her hair, untangling the knots with his fingers. She wanted to touch his head, but couldn't. The thought of it still hurt.

She loved him. She wished she'd known sooner. *A short life is a condition for love.* She'd read that somewhere, maybe in the Guest House.

Their bodies fit together perfectly. For a moment nothing else mattered. She wanted to stand that way until moss covered their limbs and birds nested in their hair. She wanted to stand that way forever.

There wasn't time. He kissed her neck and brushed the hair out of her eyes. He kissed her again, lightly, on the cheek, and then released her.

She would collapse. Her legs would not hold her. He held her at arms length and shook her again, gently.

"I love you," he said, "so put your clothes on."

She only wanted to hold him. She was too tired to care about anything else. Her body felt cold; she tried thinking about her clothes.

"When they find I'm gone they'll come after us," Christian said.

She clenched her fists and unclenched them again as nausea twisted her stomach. Her eyelids felt heavy; she doubled over to retch.

She had nothing to vomit. There was only fear inside her now and it left an acid taste on her tongue. She tried to swallow, but couldn't.

"They're not here," she said. "My clothes aren't here. I took them off. Briony has them. She said they were damp. She was afraid I'd catch pneumonia."

She sat down on the edge of the bed, unable to think clearly. Her nightgown was soaked with perspiration. Somewhere between pain and sleep she could hear her heart beating. She could hear Christian talking but his words conveyed no meaning.

"I'm going to our cabin," he said. "Can you hear me?"

She nodded.

"I'll get our things. Just a few things. I'll bring you back something to wear."

Things. Her mind flitted from thing to thing. One minute she was cold and the next she was burning with fever.

"Get some food together," he said. "Find something to eat."

Find something to eat. Bones, seeds, roots, fungus, a little of this, a little of that. She made a list in her mind. The variety was dizzying.

"If Tansy comes back, tell her you have to go outside. Go to the outhouse and wait for me. I won't be long. Can you understand me?"

She nodded, even though she didn't. The list was growing longer. There was too much to remember.

Christian tucked a blanket around her shoulders. "Okay,"

he said, "you just sit tight. I'll take care of everything. Don't worry."

She didn't say anything. She couldn't look at him.

"Matty," he said, "wait for me."

Tansy was cooking breakfast. Yarrow was crawling backwards around the room. Matty lay in bed staring out at the trees. She couldn't remember falling asleep, or if Christian had come back to wake her.

"You were dead to the world," Tansy said, "last night when I got back here. You were sitting in that chair. I had to carry you to bed."

Matty refused tea.

"If you won't let us help," said Tansy, "you'll never get well."

It was a grey morning. Large drops of rain began to pelt the roof. There was something sinister about the sound, and Tansy, despite her cheerful attempts to engage Matty in conversation, only added to the atmosphere of tension.

"Last night we had a seance," she said. "The spirits revealed something. It has to do with you." She offered Matty a large helping of lentil loaf. "Don't you want to hear about it? It has to do with your future."

Matty, hunting for some clothes, shook her head distractedly. She was concerned about Christian. For the moment no one else mattered.

Tansy threw her a pair of Stanfields. Matty changed out of her nightgown. She had slipped on a pair of gumboots and was starting towards the door when Tansy stopped her.

"Look," she said, pointing to the window. "We've got company."

Two men were leaving the Guest House. One was thin, of middle height with ragged and dirty hair falling over his broad shoulders. Most of his face was covered with hair though his beard was somewhat straggly and the outline of his chin could be clearly seen.

"That's Rasputin," said Tansy, joining Matty by the window. "He looks like a bear–furry all over. He acts like one, too, so be careful! There's no one here he hasn't tried. He'll try to take you into the bushes."

He was staring straight at them, his eyes, deep set under their bushy eyebrows, lit by a feverish intensity. He wore a knee-length tunic drawn in at the waist by a wide leather belt that buckled in front with two bear's teeth. Around his neck hung a cross made of bones.

"He never washes," Tansy continued. "It's against his religion. The Guest House will stink now. I'd advise you to stay here."

The other man was older, clean-shaven, balding. His face and body were smeared with blood, and he walked with a stoop that accentuated the grotesqueness.

"That's Hot Stuff," said Tansy. "He must have been hunting. He paints himself like that because blood has power. It's a magical link between the unknown and the known."

The men disappeared into the House of Leo. "They've come to examine Celandine's baby," said Tansy. "The Chela sent them to see if it's a boy."

"Is it?" asked Matty.

"I've been trying to tell you–Celandine had a girl. The spirits have chosen you to have the next child. They say it'll be male. The new Messiah!"

Matty opened the door, letting in a gust of wind. "The spirits are wrong," she said. "I've had my tubes tied."

"The spirits are never wrong," said Tansy. "You'll see, there'll be a miracle!"

Matty walked out into the rain. She could feel Rasputin's eyes following her across the compound, black glittering eyes that fixed her like pinpoints. Her boots were leaking; she tried to avoid the puddles. Her cold had become worse the moment she'd stepped outside.

The Guest House was empty. Christian had gone. There was no sign of his pack though his boots were standing beside the door. His old green jacket was hanging above the stove; he'd last worn it in the rain and it had dried in the shape of his body.

There was a broken bottle on the table. The room was filled with a sweet mousy smell. It was more than an unclean smell, Matty decided, though she didn't stay long enough to determine the source. She left the cabin abruptly, leaving the door ajar.

Lavender and Betony were returning from the Communal Hall with a bag of dried crowberries. Lavender had a piece of cloth she had dyed with alder bark.

"They're gifts for the Chela," explained Betony, "offerings from the new child. Briony wants to see you, by the way. She's got a message for you."

Matty walked with them as far as the House of Leo. Hot Stuff was standing in the doorway. He winked at Matty and smiled benevolently. She hurried through the rain to the House of Aries.

Briony was making huckleberry-leaf tea. "I suppose Tansy told you," she said, "about Celandine's baby. The Chela will be disappointed again. He's waited so long for a boy.

"You're our new hope," she continued, looking at Matty and smiling. "The spirits sent a message. They asked us to consider your pregnancy wishes."

"Have you seen Christian?" Matty asked. She had hoped the message would be from him. "He came last night. I was very tired. I was going to go with him but I fell asleep!"

Briony laughed. "Where would you go? You belong here, with us. But yes, I saw him, late last night. He tried to wake you. He left this note."

She handed Matty a wrinkled scrap of paper. She read the note. It was written in Christian's handwriting: *"Matty, I had to go. Six weeks at the most. I'll come back for you. Be well."*

It didn't sound like Christian. Christian wouldn't say *"be well."*

"He didn't think you were well enough to travel," said Briony. "I told him he should hike out by himself, get a boat, and then come back for you."

"But his boots," said Matty. "He left his hiking boots."

"I gave him a pair of mine," said Briony. "His soles were wearing out. They wouldn't have lasted the journey."

"He left his jacket, too," said Matty. "It's hanging up–in the Guest House."

Briony refilled Matty's cup. "From now on," she said, "you'll be staying with Tansy. The Guest House is for visitors. Rasputin and Hot Stuff are staying until the morning."

Her eyes narrowed as she studied Matty closely. "Rasputin says they met Christian on the trail. They showed him a short-cut to the river."

21

A month passed, was lost. Matty had become the centre of attention at Ephratah. She was prayed for at Prayer Breakfasts; at nightly Un-Meatings the women sang songs and danced for her. She was seldom left alone during the day, and was never allowed to leave the compound unaccompanied.

The water at the spring rose a golden rust from its source under the cedar roots; Valerian showed her how to make the drinking water more palatable by boiling it first with a small quantity of charcoal. Betony taught her how to weave cedar bark and Matty made half a rain hat. Saxifrage showed her the best place to pick fiddleheads.

From Briony she learned about the earth-star fungus and how it could forecast the weather. Tansy called it "nature's barometer." When the air was saturated the starlike rays opened up like tiny umbrellas. When the sun shone the fungus would fold itself into a tent: the rays enclosed a globular fruiting body filled with countless spores.

Gradually she was being prepared for her Pregnancy Wishes Ritual. She stopped resisting when it became clear she had no choice. She made herself believe that Christian would return, that meanwhile she must survive, must live to escape.

She was put through a period of inward purification. Her diet, controlled by Valerian, consisted of sharp-tasting foods, while Tansy made her sleep without blankets to benefit from the growth energy of the waxing moon.

At night she dreamed, waking often, nauseous, drenched in sweat. Tansy massaged her scalp and administered an emetic. She burned a sickly smelling incense which added to Matty's discomfort.

After weeks of religious and physical preparation, a message arrived from the Chela. Tansy took Matty to collect her Pregnancy Wishes baskets from each of the twelve houses. The baskets, made of birch-bark, contained fertility charms: a doll made of red cotton; a phallus-shaped cake; a D string from an old violin; feathers; antlers, claws and teeth; healing stones; medicinal plants; dyed, hand-coloured eggs stuffed with eagle-down and powdered droppings of animals; loaves of bread baked in the shape of the male and female organs conjoined in union.

At midday the women gathered inside the hall. Tansy fastened the closed baskets to the ceiling with varying lengths of string. Heartsease and Celandine decorated the room with ears of dried, painted corn and bouquets of tiny curry-smelling flowers. During the preparation of a magic circle they cast aromatic herbs on a charcoal fire burning in a small brazier, in order to attract spirits who could then take on visible shapes by enveloping themselves in the smoke.

Celandine told Matty to untie her bootlaces and anything else on her that formed a knot. "Nothing must obstruct the perfect energy flow," she said. "Don't cross your legs, or your arms, either."

The women sat down on the edge of the circle. Matty was made to stand in the centre, with a view of the infested crucifix. Replacing the head was a bleached human skull. His eyeless sockets peered back sightlessly into her own.

Briony knelt at his feet, preparing the sacrament. "This is the Chela's flesh," she said, rising to face the women. One by one they went forward to receive the sacrament then returned to their places in the circle. Briony took a piece for herself and offered the rest to Matty.

It was a fungus top, dried and wrinkled. It had a bitter, burning taste and Matty gagged as she swallowed. The previous day she had abstained from food and drink. She felt an urgent need to vomit again, but wasn't able to do so.

Briony said the feeling was caused by demons. The Chela, whose flesh they were chewing, was entering their bodies to wrestle with the dark forces. It was expected that his coming and going would be attended with painful physical and mental experiences.

Lavender produced four plates from a chest beside the altar.

"The different colours represent the four points of the compass," she explained, setting them down in their appointed positions. She placed the white plate in the north, the black one in the south, red in the west and yellow in the east.

Saxifrage made the first offering. "White is for north which is purity," she said, dropping a handful of rice into the middle of the white plate. "This is to give the child beauty of character and feature."

The plate was passed from hand to hand. Each of the women took a few grains to eat.

"Each grain is a seed gift," Saxifrage added, looking directly at Matty. Matty averted her eyes. The knot inside her was tightening.

Betony took a pouch from her pocket and sprinkled the contents onto the black plate.

"Black is south which is protection," she intoned. "We entrust the soul of this child to the Chela."

The black plate was passed around the circle. Each woman dipped a finger into the charcoal dust and made the sign of the cross on her own forehead.

Arrack stood up next, holding a coconut. She put it down in the middle of the yellow plate.

"Yellow is east which is fruition. It is the ripening inside the womb and it gives the child health." She looked at Briony, apologetically. "We had to use this ... there's no fresh fruit."

Briony picked up the coconut and passed it on to Celandine. Celandine shook it gently and pieces of dry pulp rattled against the walls of the shell.

Tansy made the last offering. She disappeared behind the altar and came out with a cage containing a young raven. Beside the bird, in a pile of black feathers, was a painted egg.

Tansy opened the cage door. The raven didn't move. Her eyes remained shut, her head hung dejectedly on her featherless breast. She'd plucked out her feathers to make the nest for the egg. It was the only sign of life, Tansy said, she'd shown in captivity.

Tansy took the egg and placed it at Matty's feet. "Step on it," she ordered. "It will cast off any evil spirits that live in your clothes."

Before Matty could respond, Tansy stepped on the egg and crushed it. The raven opened one eye and blinked.

"See," said Briony, spooning the broken egg into a cup, "your clothes were infested. The evil has been driven away. You can get undressed now. You must be completely naked."

It was cold and damp in the hall. Sensing Matty's reluctance, Briony laid an icy hand on her elbow. The fingers closed, claw-like, threatening. Matty fumbled with the buttons on her shirt.

She unzipped her jeans and Briony released her. Matty stripped and stood naked in front of the women. She had the strange sensation of feeling hot and cold simultaneously. Colours were intensified. Her brain became an echo chamber where all things dissolved in laughter.

Briony took a knife and wiped it with a cloth. She ran her thumb down the full length of the blade, testing for sharpness.

Tansy lifted off the roof of the cage. Briony grabbed the

raven by its feet and swung it up into the air. She held it over Matty's head while the other women began chanting. Something cold and wet dripped out of the bird's mouth.

Spittle, Matty thought, as the slime travelled down over her scalp. She'd watched ravens mating; she'd seen the male fly up and then plunge earthwards towards his mate. When he reached her they tumbled together while he filled her mouth with his spit. Dan said the female was impregnated that way.

The chant had begun as a moan and had changed into a song. It filled Matty's head with echoes and vibrations. The bird hung upside down over her head. She could feel the liquid dribbling onto her face and neck.

The women were chanting faster, working themselves into a frenzy. Some of them spoke in tongues, chirping and muttering as the spirits sent indecipherable messages, while others repeated their mantras in voices that were barely audible.

Briony took the bird by the neck and pinned its head to the floor. Its eyes bulged as it struggled to free itself, wings flapping, and small cries drowned in the deafening clamour.

Briony twisted its neck with one hand, wringing it like a dishcloth. Its beak opened, and blood dripped out.

The colours of the blood, like oil-paint and water mixed, were terrifying to see. Matty looked at the bird, then looked quickly away.

Briony raised her hand and the noise stopped. There was a moment of silence while she paused to catch her breath.

Taking hold of the knife, she raised it high above her head. She brought it down hard on the raven's neck: the head flew into the air, blood shooting out in all directions.

"Blood," said Tansy, "for the west which is strength." Briony handed her the coconut which she had neatly cut in half with the same knife. Tansy held the bird over the shell letting the blood run into it until it was nearly full. She mixed in the broken egg, stirring it around with her finger. Saxifrage added a handful of rice, Betony a pinch of charcoal.

The shell was passed around the room; the women dipped their fingers into the blood and traced the sign of the cross on their foreheads.

Matty was made to lie on her back, spreadeagled. Her hands and feet were secured with heavy thongs. Betony knelt over her and drew charcoal circles around her breasts. Arrack traced the circles in blood while Saxifrage sprinkled rice over the floor. They drew lines across her stomach with charcoal, traced her pubic area in blood. They painted her face with blood, her teeth with charcoal.

Seconds went by. Outside Matty could hear the children laughing. When she closed her eyes she saw the torture tree, the children not laughing but crying. A dark blue fluid dripped from their eyes. *Was she screaming outwardly or only inside her head?*

Minutes passed, whole hours were lost. Someone was drumming on her stomach, on her belly about to erupt like Popocatepetl. Spewing up farmers, ruining crops. Her belly was a black hole, a hole full of earth.

Someone was chanting, someone was dancing. It was a devil dancing, a giant cock. Flies swarmed stupefied around the milky tip. Behind Matty's eyes there were blinding flashes of light.

Was she laughing outwardly or only to herself?

Her head felt as empty as the coconut of fruition. She could hear a voice, the hollow voice of her mother crying *sexual intercourse sexual intercourse sexual intercourse!* She was back inside the womb again, screaming to get out. *Was she screaming inside the womb or only inside herself?*

Her mouth was a black hole, gritty. The earth: had she eaten it?

Someone was rubbing her belly. She felt the seed-gift inside her bursting into life–an egg full of anger, full of broken red hearts.

You've got to eat, said her father.

Face it, Dan said, *you'll die.*

Memory, a black hole. *I love you*, said Christian, *put your clothes on.*

Someone was eating her from the inside out. Deep in her womb she felt the trap, heard a trapped animal in her wild raving. She saw the skinned body covered with flies. She heard the tired jaws breaking.

A grotesque gnome in the centre of a stone. The stone a brain. Whose brain? Who is who? Her brain, a grave with a woman asleep in it. A wreath for a bridal, a sad bouquet.

Knots in her side, in her groin, in her belly. She'd been spayed flayed, payed, made. Sighs and whispers. Ladies and gentlemen, a perfect specimen.

Laughter. "Life is much more fun when you're refreshed."

More laughter. "And death refreshes you best."

Stitches in her side, in her groin, in her belly. The operation when she was five times three times two take away seven.

She opened her eyes. Had they always been closed? The Pregnancy Wishes basket swung over her head. Deep inside she felt the one knot that could never be undone, the final obstruction. The baskets grinned down, mysterious and all-knowing. She wanted to break them apart. She wanted to breathe the clean sky. She felt as if the floor were giving way beneath her. She was sinking into a vault like a finished pelt.

Her eyes were heavy as coins. They were making her drink. No, it was only her own spit. They were trying to smother her instead. No, they were trying to wipe away the hurt.

She had drooled like an idiot. Incontinent. Her body was dripping: blue fluid, red worms. She was riding a cock horse to Banbury Cross. She was cradled in the bosom of the deep.

Titters. She was in the middle of an ocean making love to a captain. She was the ship, he was the first-class swimming pool. She could walk, she could wink, she could talk, she could sink. The captain was a doll himself only slightly less human.

The captain took her hand. He put it in a jar. The hand grew fins and became a fish. She swallowed him like the ocean.

When she came to, it was dark. A heavy cloud of sulphurous fumes lingered over the hall. Tansy lit a stick of incense and placed it beside her head. Around her bed there were seven candles burning.

The light was dazzling. Matty sat up, shielding her eyes. Her stomach heaved, it was empty. Her body ached. Her head was throbbing.

"You're alive!" Tansy gasped, unable to hide her amazement. "I thought you were . . . I thought they'd killed you!"

Matty groaned, shifting onto her side on the hard pallet. "Who?" she asked. "What are you talking about?"

"The demons. They possessed you. The Chela is supposed to exorcise them when you eat the sacrament. You ate the sacrament but then you started raving."

"What demons?" asked Matty. The bad taste in her mouth persisted and the back of her throat felt raw.

"The demons inside you. We had to burn brimstone to drive them out. That's what the smell is. Briony also gave you a dose of asafoetida."

"I was hallucinating," said Matty. "After that I don't remember."

"You were vomiting," said Tansy. "It was all beautiful colours. You've been out ever since. I thought you hadn't made it."

Tansy told her about the actual conception, how it wasn't necessary to be conscious for the duration. The Chela appeared in his earthly body to consummate the Wishes by sexual intercourse. Matty looked amazed.

"We didn't stay for that part," Tansy added hastily. "The

Chela doesn't like an audience. Briony was with you the whole time, though. She has to make sure the ceremony is completed."

"I can't get pregnant," Matty insisted. "It's impossible. I've already told you. I had an operation."

"Of course you can," said Tansy, "just think about it. I thought *I* was sterile, too. Before I came to Ephratah."

Matty shook her head. She felt as if her vital organs had been cut out, surgically bandaged, and put back in the wrong order. Her heart was beating in the pit of her stomach. Her liver and lungs had exchanged places.

"There's no point in worrying," said Tansy, "it's already happened. Now you're like the earth-star fungus. The ripe, fruiting body."

She carried a basin over to the bed and began washing Matty's head with water in which seven leaves of different plants had been shredded. The water, she said, was medicinal. It was a medium through which helpful spirits could enter her head and fight off any remaining evil.

She returned to the woodstove where something was cooking. She removed the lid of the pot and Matty caught a whiff of herbs, a relief from the powerful sulphur-fumes and incense.

"It's stew," said Tansy, bringing it to the table. "Celandine prepared it."

Matty climbed out of bed. Her body was seized by another bout of dry-retching.

"You must get some food into you," Tansy repeated, dishing a small amount into a wooden bowl. "Besides, it's an important part of the Ritual, this stew. It was made especially for you."

Celandine and Arrack came in the door. Both of them looked surprised to see Matty at the table.

"Briony sent us to clean up," said Celandine, regaining her composure. She had a constant loving smile, a gaze aimed two inches behind the subject's eyes. "She would have come herself but she's still with the Chela."

"Someone's using voodoo," said Arrack. "The Chela was nearly crushed. It happened after we'd left – when he'd come for the conception. The skull fell off the crucifix and part of the altar collapsed."

"I don't know what you're talking about," said Tansy, her lips tightening. Arrack turned pale.

Matty looked at the altar but the crucifix was gone. In its place there was something that looked like a scarecrow, made from dried branches and leaves, and dressed in Matty's clothing.

"It's almost midnight," said Celandine, looking from the effigy to where Matty was sitting. "Has Tansy told you about the Manger?"

"She's just woken up," said Tansy, hastily. "She's going to eat some of your stew. Are either of you hungry? There's plenty of food."

"Nobody has an appetite tonight," said Arrack, hurriedly. "Wishing takes a lot of energy. We need sleep, not food."

Matty looked at the stew. She didn't feel hungry, either. She took a small mouthful to appease Tansy. There was something in the stew besides vegetables, something slimy and indisguisable, like octopus.

"If you can't chew it, just swallow," said Tansy. "It gets a bit stringy sometimes. I might have overcooked it."

Devil-fish, Matty thought, not stopping to consider the unlikelihood of such a prospect: she'd come to expect anything at Ephratah. She tried to swallow, Grannie Gull-like, without chewing. The food caught in her throat and would go no further.

She remembered following Dan, bleach bottle in hand, at low tide to catch octopus. He squirted the bleach under a rock, and when an octopus came out he stuck it with a crowbar right through the brain. He objected to her calling it *brain* when *head* would have been enough. *Brain* seemed more dramatic at the time.

Violet hung the octopus on a hook in the rafters. It twitched up there for hours refusing to die, and later, when Matty was making supper, it fell to the floor and began inching towards the door. Spaghetti Chops slipped on it when he staggered in, drunk.

Arrack thumped Matty across the back. She swallowed. Her stomach sent queasy messages to her brain and she pushed the bowl away.

"It's your last chance to eat," said Tansy. She scraped the stew back into the pot. "Celandine is taking you to the Manger. You must stay there alone for the next two days. While you're there you have to fast. Deprivation is essential to the spiritual growth of the foetus."

Celandine took Matty's hand. "It's a quiet space for your thoughts," she said. "You'll feel fine, once you get used to it."

Matty welcomed the chance to be on her own. Unlike the others she did not find solitude disorienting.

She stood up, supporting herself on the table. She could feel the stew, a dead weight in her stomach, as Celandine took her arm and steered her towards the door. They made their way through the darkness.

"There's an outhouse around the back," Celandine told her as they approached the Manger, "but don't leave the house for any other reason. There's lots of dry wood inside. We lit a fire this morning. Don't forget – you can't talk to anyone. There's fresh water in that bucket. That's all you can have to drink."

Celandine opened the door; the room was lit with candles. There were no decorations as there'd been in the Guest House, no books on the shelves, nothing to suggest comfort.

Celandine sat down on a stool beside the stove. "There's one more thing I have to tell you," she said. "In case you get in any trouble and can't cope with it on your own, I want to give you the formula so you can make yourself invisible."

It was Arrack's formula, Celandine said, and only to be

used in an emergency. Like all spells it could be dangerous; Rosemary had misused it and she'd disappeared forever.

"First you must take off all your clothes. Then you must visualize an imaginary door. You must stand in front of this door, with your arms outstretched like a cross, and say to yourself: *In the midst of life we are in death.* Say these words three times, and the third time mentally impress the words on the door. If the spell has worked the door will swing open. Then you can pass through it and on the other side you'll be invisible.

"It's simple," she said, "there's really nothing to it. It's magic–like giving birth is magic. This is your first experience?"

Matty couldn't speak. Celandine took her hand and pressed it against her own soft belly.

"It's so sensual. When your belly swells and your breasts fill up with milk, you feel like a whole person."

Matty sat down on the bed. Celandine sat down beside her, undoing her jacket and opening her shirt. "Look," she said, taking out a breast and squeezing the nipple. "Did you ever see anything like it?"

After she left Matty added more wood to the fire. She lit another candle and went to the outhouse.

Her mouth, full of grit, tasted like a compost heap. She rinsed it with water but her teeth were coated in slime.

She sat down on the doorstep and stared out into the night. She thought of Dan again, how he wore his toothbrush around his neck as if it were a good luck charm. Always a blue toothbrush, she remembered. Hers had never been anything but yellow.

She wanted her toothbrush. She'd meant to ask for it. She'd seen it sitting on the table at the Communal Hall along with all her other possessions. The candles gave off a musky scent, inducing a comfortable drowsiness, and she decided to return to the Communal Hall before sleep took her over.

It was well after midnight. There were no lights burning in

any of the cabins as Matty crept through the blackness, shielding her candle from the rising breeze. She stopped outside the Guest House, wondering if the Chela were in there sleeping. The thought frightened her. She started walking faster.

The candle spluttered and died. She stood still for a moment, adjusting her eyes to the darkness. The Communal Hall lay in the clearing up ahead. She groped her way towards it.

The door was unlocked. She went inside, feeling about for the matches usually kept on the windowsill above the counter. Locating a jar, she reached down into it. She withdrew her hand, disgustedly. She'd touched something slippery and wet.

She felt further along the windowsill, discovered another jar and opened it. Reaching in, cautiously this time, she found a handful of matches. She lit the candle, but all her things were gone. She was about to leave when she remembered the first jar and turned, hesitantly, to examine it.

The jar contained the remains of the stew. It was plainly labelled: CELANDINE'S AFTERBIRTH FOR PREGNANCY WISHES.

"Placenta," Tansy had told Matty, weeks ago when discussing the dietary laws of Ephratah. "That's the one meat you can eat without having to kill it."

22

Matty lay awake all night. Virgin, Wife, Lover, Mother: she felt remote from everything earthly.

Virgin was for the South, for Childhood and Purity. Wife was for the West, East Oyster and Futility. Lover was for the East, the Unknown and Mystery. Mother was for the North, for Ephratah and Fertility.

She curled into the foetal position. It was getting light; she wished it would stay dark forever. She pulled a blanket over her head. There was no way to shut out the awareness that came with morning.

She drifted, half delirious, into a realm of shadows. Colours didn't exist, sounds were muted. Voices buzzed faintly in her ear. Everything she touched was without substance.

She was sitting in a graveyard with her mother and Aunt Dot. The graves were strewn with flowers; the flowers gave off no scent.

Her mother opened a picnic basket. She set out a lacquered tray with a red and white checkered pattern. She decorated the squares with sandwiches and cakes. Matty lost her appetite. Her mother opened a tiny box.

"Look what I've got," she whispered. It was her heart.

Aunt Dot began to cough. Her flesh sagged, her ribs stuck out brittle as pencils. She smiled an artificial smile.

"That's nothing," she said simply. "I've got a bigger

one!" She rummaged about in her shopping bag. An amber mist, cool as dusk, settled over the graves. "Oh dear," she gasped, clutching the bag to her hollow chest, "my heart is broken! I'll have to die."

"Good-bye," said Matty, coldly. Tears had come to her mother's eyes. "Real tears?" asked Matty.

Her mother nodded: "See, I'm still alive."

Young Woman, Old Woman, Dead Woman, Ghost.

Matty was making love to Briony. Briony was covered in soft brown fur. She had a trap between her legs and Matty was caught, head first. "Eat," Briony ordered. "Eat your way out!"

Matty ate a piece of cake. She ate a sandwich. Her mother closed the picnic basket. Matty's appetite increased.

She ate a handful of earth. She ate dead flowers. She began to eat her hands and her feet. Blood dripped from her mouth; the blood was tasteless.

She woke with a start. Pain, a slow hand, gripped her body, clenched into a fist and twisted inside. The pain was familiar: every month it came. Soon she would bleed. Outside the earth-star would open.

She turned onto her back and gazed out the window. The sun was rising; a hundred yellow birds shed their feathers over the trees.

The pain was constant, immobilizing. She was grateful, almost, for this tangible reminder of her existence.

Sunlight caught the dew on the trees and grasses. There were no yellow birds, no feathers – she'd imagined them.

Imagination, Briony had told her, was a tool of Satan. "The devil pollutes the minds of independent thinkers. The Chela will do your thinking for you."

Matty closed her eyes. She tried to imagine the Chela.

She awoke. The door was open, the room smelled like rotten eggs. She sat up and rubbed the sleep from her eyes. A figure loomed over the foot of her bed.

One half of the body glowed, the other was lost in darkness. The luminous side, radiating warmth and life, was almost transparent. The dark side was cold, massive, sinister-looking.

He was exactly as Tansy described him: a spiritual master reconciled to every aspect of "The All" in himself–evil and good, hate and love, cruelty and affection, tears and laughter.

He was dressed in a white hooded robe gathered at the waist by a metal belt engraved with the signs of the zodiac. Over his heart was a Nazi Death's Head in the shape of a skull and crossbones. He wore bracelets studded with gold nuggets and rings of emerald and turquoise.

A Divine Being, a Glorious Power, the Centre, the Chela. His presence filled the room, and Matty, propped between two pillows, felt her body beginning to shake. His presence filled her head. All sound became his breathing, all silence her heartbeat.

The whole room was shaking. He was approaching her, moving around to the side of the bed. Suddenly he seemed smaller–the two halves of his body had united into a different reality, that of a short fat dwarf.

He was nothing like she had imagined. He had been standing on the woodbox to make himself tall. His head was exceptionally large, his eyes puffy and bloodshot. The nose, a shade redder than the rest of his face, was small and snubbed. Lips and chin were hidden under a profusion of hair.

He stroked his beard with stumpy, hairy fingers. He stared at her, his face showing signs of agitation. Matty stared back; the eye-contact made him jittery. He shook off his hood and scratched his balding head. His hair was matted, a dirty yellow.

She tried to empty her mind, frightened by the grotesque image. Briony said that an image, when held in the mind with sufficient clarity, could be projected onto the mental spheres of others. Matty did not want *him* to see what she saw.

He was breathing heavily. She could hear the sound of her blood. Somebody was calling her. In the back of her head she could hear voices.

"The human voice," he said, unexpectedly, "is the most potent sound on earth. Human blood provides nourishment for the sun. Human breath is part of the divine current. We carry within us, you see, the wonders we seek without."

He bent over and kissed her forehead. He made the sign of the cross with his saliva. Matty noticed the large growth protruding from his right nostril. It had sprouted four hairs, each a different colour: black, white, red, yellow. His front teeth were made of gold and the sun sign of Sagittarius, a miniature hammer and sickle, was tattooed on his forehead.

"Let me introduce myself properly," he continued. "The last time we met I believe you were under my influence."

He giggled, mechanically, as if his voice box were attached by a string to a cord at the base of his neck, a string that he could pull to produce pre-recorded speech or laughter. His whole body shook when he laughed. He was more goblinesque than dwarf-like.

"You're right again," he quipped, taking a little step backwards. "I am not a normal man. In fact, as you'll see, I am not a man at all. I am an all-encompassing Divine Power."

He coughed and cleared his throat like an ordinary person discharging yin. There were flabby folds of skin under his eyes; he looked as if he had spent a week without sleep.

"Other men say, 'I am a body and I possess a soul,' but I say, 'I am a soul and I possess a body.' I am beyond sin, so any woman joining with me cannot sin either."

He closed his eyes and bowed his head, his bald spot a small round lake in a forest.

"I am your God and my body is your temple. As the flower turns to the sun that the bright beams may aid in perfecting its beauty and symmetry, so should you turn to my Glorious Radiance that heaven's light may shine upon us, that your character may be developed in the likeness of my own."

He made the sign of the cross again and retreated into the far corner of the room. He closed the door and lit a fire in the stove, feeding it with hemlock, henbane, coriander, and sandalwood. The room filled with the smoke, a powerful narcotic. Matty covered her head with a pillow. Her feeling of nausea was returning.

The Chela sat down, crosslegged, on the end of her bed. He reached into a pocket and pulled out a small reedy instrument. He seemed oblivious to the smoke though Matty could barely breathe. The smoke enveloped her; she began to hallucinate.

She could hear organ music. A fat creature with wings opened a bottle marked SUPER THICK HAIR IN ONLY FIVE SECONDS. Matty took a sip. Her hair became a nest; birds with human faces were flying around her head.

The Chela began to play. The sound hurt her ears. His flute was a knife, a drill, a hammer. The music wounded her, bore into her, pounded inside her brain.

The pain worked its way down the length of her body. It was *her* pain: she owned it. The Chela was trying to take it away. He wanted to control her, to possess her through his music.

The heavily perfumed air made breathing impossible. Matty burned; flames danced in circles before her eyes. She tried to free herself but the smoke was too dense. She struggled and cried aloud. The Chela was going to choke her.

"Relax," he was saying in a voice not human. "I'm only trying to help you. Calm down, please. Try to breathe."

He set aside his instrument, slipped his hand under her sweater and massaged her belly. The pain was hiding there; it gnawed like a rat. The hand was drumming, probing, soothing. The pain went deeper: her own pain, precious.

He was chanting again, a spell against barrenness. It was no good, she was all emptiness. His fingers drummed to the rhythm of the chant. He wouldn't relax her, she'd keep on resisting.

"Are you musical?" he asked, a stupid question. How could she answer when her mouth was full of smoke?

No, her mouth was frozen. She'd made a mistake. Anyone could make the same mistake under pressure.

It was the *pain* that was frozen, not her mouth. There was always a pain *somewhere.* Pain of the spirit, pain of the flesh: there was no way to distinguish between the two.

She started to cry. That felt better. He was smiling over her, beatific. He was drumming out his message and somewhere inside her the answer was writhing.

She was sobbing quite openly now, she had no more energy to fight him. In the distance she could hear the wind. The room smelled fresh and fragrant.

"That's better. You're doing fine. I've opened the window. Take a deep breath. That's the way."

He stroked her small hands clasped childlike under her chin. No more pain, no more claw, no more tearing. There was only a dull ache. The Chela had taken away her pain.

He picked up the flute and lifted it to his lips. The music began again, the music of angels.

Two men were hunting in the room. Matty hid under the bed, her knife poised. One man stepped outside leaving the other alone. She waited until he'd fallen asleep; she slit a wide grin from one side of his throat to the other.

Blood gushed out like water from a bilge pump. Blood on her hands, all over the walls. Blood on the bed, on Celandine's blanket. She'd have to wash the blood away. She'd have to get rid of the body.

She woke lying in a pool of her own blood. Her period had started. She lay still for a moment wondering what to do. A fire was blazing in the stove and someone was doing push-ups in the middle of the floor.

She looked at him in horror, remembering who he was. He was breathing irregularly and raindrops of sweat had formed on his brow. He looked up when he heard the bed creak. His overalls had split in the crotch.

"You fell asleep on me last night," he puffed. "Don't let it worry you. Say, are you feeling better this morning? I thought you had an appendicitis!"

Matty groaned. "I've got my period," she said. "There's blood all over the sheets." Her voice sounded calm but inside she was trembling. Tears had formed in the corners of her eyes. She blinked, stifling the cry that was rising in her throat.

The Chela began to cough. He had difficulty catching his breath. He struggled to his feet, his face colouring. "Smoking," he rasped. "It's a killer."

He mopped his forehead with a polka-dot hankie and sat down beside her on the bed. "You wouldn't happen to have an old butt on you, by any chance?"

Matty shook her head. "What arc you going to do with me? I told them I wouldn't get pregnant!"

She was unable to restrain her tears any longer. The Chela began chewing at a hangnail.

"I don't suppose you have any Tampax, either," he said, looking at her helplessly. "We better make something for you out of that sheet. Something to plug you up with."

He seemed strangely unconcerned about her condition. She'd expected him to be angry but instead he seemed almost embarrassed.

"It's only a bit of blood," he said. "Of course we men have no idea. I did know a man who bled sympathetically–from the rectum. He died in the end. Cancer, I think."

He passed Matty his hankie and she blew her nose. He helped her to her feet, dabbing at her eyes with the corner of the bloodied sheet. "Come on now, we'll get you cleaned up. Please stop crying. We've got a bad enough mess to deal with down below."

He tore the sheet in half and folded it into a rectangle. He asked if she had any safety pins to make diapers; she had nothing and he made a pair anyway, tying them on her with knots.

He gave her the gown he'd been wearing the night before. "Now we should eat," he said. "The body needs fuel in a time of crisis."

The blood on her face felt cold and sticky. She'd come full circle from the Pregnancy Wishes Ritual. She was meant to be alone now, meant to be fasting. *Deprivation was essential* . . . but there'd never be any foetus.

"You can't have everything," said the Chela, rubbing his plump belly. "If you can't have a baby you might as well have breakfast. How about some sausages? A couple of fried eggs? Look, tell me something. What did you say your name was?"

"Amaranth," said Matty. "It's the name Betony gave me."

"Not *that* one. Your *real* name. You told me last night but I don't remember names. Faces, they're different. I never forget a face."

"It's Matty," she said, "short for Martha. My father's idea. He thought it sounded solid."

"It sounds sea-worthy," said the Chela. "Don't tell me, let me guess! Your father was hoping you'd be a boat?"

He grinned and Matty laughed.

"Never mind," he said, unpacking his knapsack, "nobody's perfect. How do you like your sausage? Sunny-side up?"

"I haven't eaten meat for ages," said Matty, her face growing serious again. "You know what Briony says. She thinks it makes people aggressive."

"She's nuts! I eat meat three times a day myself. If I didn't I'd faint. Briony's always been a fanatic. Don't take anything she says too seriously."

The Chela seemed to have changed overnight. He'd become much less divine since she'd caught him at his exercises.

"Listen," he said, "do you mind if I call you Matty. That's

the easiest. You can call me Stan. It's short for the Glorious Power."

"Stan?" said Matty.

"You Matty, me Stan. Call me anything you like but just don't call me late for breakfast!" He collapsed with mirth, clutching his paunch as if it might fall off. Matty laughed too. His good humour was infectious.

He spread his supplies on the table: sausages, eggs, bread, butter, flour, sugar, marmalade, instant coffee, a small skillet, plate, cup, knife, fork, spoon, salt and pepper. "Chocolate," he said, reaching down into the bottom of his pack. "I never travel without it. Of course Briony doesn't know. She'd kill me. She thinks eating chocolate is worse than murder."

Now seemed the right moment to ask the question. "Does Briony know you're here?" said Matty.

The Chela looked at her thoughtfully. "I like you," he said, "but you're too smart. I can see I'm going to have to be straight with you."

"She sent you?" Matty asked.

"She told me about you. Both of us feel you'd be better off . . . you're different from the others. You don't belong here. Briony knew that the moment she laid eyes on you. I can see it too. You have a great future ahead of you."

The Chela wanted Matty to live in his camp. She could stay there as his "female counterpart," the Real Mother (her role would be entirely asexual, he assured her) "helping to fulfill God's plan for creation."

"Face it," said the Chela, "we have to keep up appearances. For the sake of the other women at least. Briony's the only one who knows the real truth about me. If you want to come along, I'll tell you the whole tale."

Matty expressed concern over Christian's story. The Chela said Rasputin had straightened everything out.

"It was all a big misunderstanding," he said. "Christian had the wrong idea about us. He's coming to see you when he gets another boat. If you want to go back with him then, you're free."

He dropped an egg into the skillet, splattering himself with grease. "How much can you eat?" he asked. "One egg or three?"

"One," said Matty. "Are you sure he's going to come back?"

"He left you this note," said the Chela. "I almost forgot."

"Matty. Disregard previous message. Everything o.k. Will meet you at the charcoal burners' camp one month's time. Christian."

"The last note said six weeks," said Matty. "A month's already gone by."

The Chela looked at her, and sighed. "What is time?" He chuckled to himself and slid two eggs onto the tin plate. "Here, eat this. It'll put some hair on your breath."

Matty sat down across from him and picked at her breakfast. The Chela, watching her, picked at his wart.

She pushed the sausages to one side.

"Protein," he said, "that's your problem. Not enough protein to keep a fly alive."

Matty wasn't hungry.

"How's about I make some of that instant coffee. I don't know about you but I'm a regular junkie." He belched. "Trouble with sausages is they go straight through. I'll be back in a flush. I'm going outside."

While he was gone she scraped her plate. She ate a piece of toast with butter and marmalade, and made a cup of coffee in the lightweight aluminum cup.

She knew she was going with him; it had already been decided. She reread the note from Christian and tossed it into the fire.

Part Five
The Charcoal Burners' Camp

23

"I always wanted to be a soldier," said the Chela as he led her across the muskeg. "They took one look at me and laughed. I couldn't even get a job cleaning toilets."

It was rough going over the spongy ground. Matty was exhausted and they'd only come three miles from Ephratah. She was tired of walking, tired of listening. The Chela's steady pace was as relentless as his monologue.

"Sure, I was going to be great. I told myself, someday wherever I go, when people hear my name, they'll know who I am. Like Hitler. You know, the Austrian Army rejected *him* once for being too weak. As far as I'm concerned, his only weakness was his vegetarianism!"

The Chela had grown up in a carnival. "Some kids think it's a big deal," he said. "They want to run away from home, you know, and join the circus." They'd stopped to rest and he was eating a fried-egg sandwich. "Well, I spent my whole life trying to run away from *it.*"

Riding the carnival train, setting up bingo and side-shows and rigged galleries to fleece the suckers, working eighteen hours a day in mud or heat – this was all he could remember of his early childhood.

"I was a natural carny," he said, "a freak. The only time I ever saw myself was in those, you know, distorting mirrors. I thought I looked normal. I was surrounded by creeps anyways, like giants and contortionists. We all thought the *rest* of the world was weird.

"My old man was a hustler, he ran the whole show. My mother, she kept the family together. I can still see her tripping over the slop bucket I was supposed to have emptied, mouthful of clothespins, saying 'shit shit shit,' and the old man yelling 'don't tell me your troubles I got a load of my own.'

"We were piss-poor," he continued, taking a large bite of his third sandwich, "lived on flour and grease and all the stale popcorn we could scrounge after a show. The locals never liked us – always the carnies versus the townies – and they made that clear. I think they hated us because we came out at night. Like prostitutes, pimps, that sort of thing."

He paused to break wind. "Jeezus-gloriosky! It's some sob story when you come to think about it. Say, you're not eating anything. How's about sharing the rest of my sandwich?"

Matty shook her head. She'd had enough to eat at breakfast and the greasy, half-eaten sandwich didn't appeal to her.

"Now, what was I saying? You following me so far? It's not often I get a chance like this. Your friends, you know how it is, they've heard the story before and they're sick of it.

"So anyway, the older I got, the more curious I got. About the outside world that is. My old man didn't like that. He needed me for the circus. My mother used to sneak me pocketbooks and I'd stay awake all night reading them.

"For my birthday one year she gave me a camera. I think she stole it for me. Just a cheap thing, nothing special. But I got some film and took a bunch of pictures – rotten ropes, torn canvas, hobos, roughies, tough town people, weirdos and queers. I got a good beating when my old man found out. The last thing he wanted was an artist in the family.

"So I ran away. The police brought me back. It's the only time the police ever sided with my father. Ennis, Montana. The old man sold the camera."

They set out again over the muskeg. The Chela kept on

talking and Matty had to run to keep up with him.

After his return to the circus he'd worked for three weeks pulling nails out of boards. "It was months before I'd redeemed myself–before the old man gave me a decent job." A freak clown to shovel the hot manure, he'd tripped around the ring after the ballerina on her horse.

Hot Stuff, a firebreather, joined the show in North Dakota. "One day he showed me all his scars. He had scabs and blisters everywhere and he'd lost a hand, too. I think he was some kind of a repressed arsonist. When he started burning charcoal he stopped setting fire to himself!"

Hot Stuff introduced them to Reptile, "a real brain." Reptile operated the snake show but at night he sat alone making robots. "He knew something about electricity so my old man let him wire the Headless Woman. The chair she sat in was badly made and one day she got electrocuted. The old man was a real bastard to work for."

Rasputin, a lapsed Buddhist, joined the carnival as a hypnotist. He would hypnotize people and empty their wallets. He staged satanic orgies in his tent at night under the pretext of some phoney religion, and took particular pleasure in young girls. Eventually the police raided and the carnival shut down.

"My old man was ruined–he's dead now and it doesn't matter–and Rasputin went to jail. Hot Stuff and I came to Canada."

They separated at the border. The Chela went to Toronto where he got a job in a camera shop.

"The owner had a son, a Mongoloid idiot. I think I was hired to keep the little creep company."

The Chela worked in the back of the shop and learned to repair cameras. The idiot, whose name was Beefy, played at his feet, dribbling. In the evenings they watched television together. They shared the same bedroom, too, sleeping on bunkbeds barely wide enough to support skeletons, and Beefy would sing television commercials in his sleep. His favourite was about wanting to be an Oscar-Meyer Weiner because then everyone would be in love with him.

A year went by and the Chela learned his trade. When a sample photograph accompanied a malfunctioning camera, he would often invent a story to fit the face. During the time he worked he learned one thing about people. Most of them could not look a camera in the eye.

The Chela had a talent for manipulating people. He practised on Beefy, a particularly reliable victim. He would penetrate him with a look meant to undo any remote feeling of well-being the boy might have, and then order him to carry out some pointless task such as dusting lens caps on all the unrepaired cameras or sorting through the waste basket for invisible parts of a mechanism more often than not of his own invention.

Mrs. Beefy had a soft spot in her heart for freaks. With her, the Chela took a more subtle approach. When she ironed his clothes or made his bed in the morning he would come to her, overwhelmed with gratitude and love. No one had even noticed her before, let alone been so appreciative. The Chela soon had her eating out of his hands.

He waited awhile before deciding the best method of handling Beefy's father. He reminded the Chela of his own father, with his pinched mouth and beak of a nose. Mean little eyes that saw right through you and out the other side. Coarse, horny hands from a lifetime of handling money.

Money was his main weakness. He had thousands. Beefy was another weakness, his only son.

The Chela lavished affection on the boy, doting on him like a brother. Mr. Beefy took them out together to a soccer match one bitter Saturday afternoon. It was the first time he had dared to appear in public with his miserable offspring and the dwarf handyman. He explained to his friends that he had hired the little man through an organization for the handicapped, that despite all appearances he was a good repairman. The Chela bought Beefy an ice-cream cone; Beefy crammed it into his ear. Mr. Beefy made him wait in the car after that, determined to carry on till the end of the game.

The Chela did not socialize much in Toronto. Once he ventured into a body-rub parlour where a half-naked woman half-heartedly rubbed his back.

"The city was no place for a dwarf with no money. If you're not normal, I told myself, you've got to be rich!" He stopped in his tracks and Matty almost collided with him. "We're home," he said. "Take a whiff."

Matty sniffed. There was a piercing, rank, sour smell in the air. The Chela pointed into the trees where a thin blue wisp of smoke hung in the low branches, as if a spirit had dissolved, leaving its last breath.

"They're burning a kiln," he said. "Look, over there!"

The light was fading. The dark kiln, rising out of the centre of the clearing, looked like a smouldering circus tent. Two dark figures moved noiselessly among the shadows, like wood demons. They stopped to nod at the Chela, and one of them – the other she recognized as Hot Stuff – waved at Matty through the smoky haze.

"That's Reptile," said the Chela. "He and Hot Stuff always work together."

Around the kiln, like stars circling the sun, small fires were burning to light up the clearing. The place had a ghostly atmosphere, and Matty turned to look over her shoulder when they'd passed, wondering if it had been some fantasy.

The camp itself, in contrast to the clearing, was dismally unromantic. It had nothing of Ephratah's symmetry but was simply a collection of run-down buildings dotted about on skids over the mud. They reminded Matty of the bunkhouses at East Oyster. There was even a cookhouse set further back in the trees, a scattering of rusty machinery, a defunct generator, a repair shop and saw mill and a number of storage sheds.

Nobody came out to greet them though Matty could hear laughter coming from one of the shacks. The Chela motioned her to follow him, and they continued past the cookhouse deeper into the woods.

"I thought you could use some privacy," said the Chela, "being a lady and all. The men don't come up here that much. I think you'll like the place. Designed it myself."

To the right of the path, set a few feet into the bush, two cedar saplings had been bent towards one another and fastened at the top to form an arch. Beyond this gateway lay a small hut made from cedar poles packed with cedar boughs, moss, and earth. It was badly pushed out of shape; the walls bulged in every direction.

"Don't worry. It's sturdy," said the Chela. "I built it for the Messiah. It gets a bit drafty but these spiritual types don't seem to notice. He hasn't returned to earth yet anyway – at least not physically. I've decided to stay here myself until he does."

There was no furniture in the room other than a bed. It was made from poles and brushwood, covered with cedar boughs and ferns.

"The bed's for you," he said. "I use the floor. Too much luxury can make a person soft. Besides, I've got my own padding!" He giggled, waggling his bottom. "No sense dieting, I always say to myself. Enjoy life while you can!"

He giggled again. He seemed immensely pleased with himself as he strutted about the bare room making sure all was in order.

"How's about I rustle us up some grub," he said. "You get a fire going. There's a sack of charcoal out back. You'll need some kindling, too. I'll be right back."

He left her collecting dry twigs and pitch-wood, and when he returned, with marshmallows, a package of chocolate chip cookies, a pound of cheese, and a bottle of wine, Matty had a fire burning.

"Good work!" he exclaimed, spreading the food out on the floor. "You're the first person who hasn't filled the place with smoke. What do you say we toast some marshmallows?

I've had a craving for them lately, myself."

He went outside and cut two toasting sticks from a young alder. The dirt floor was cold; Matty scraped together a pile of leaves and sat down on them.

"So," said the Chela, sharpening his stick, "I said to myself if you can't be good-looking, get rich. Here I am today. Couldn't be better."

Matty rescued a marshmallow from the flames.

"I'll have that one," said the Chela. "I like them well done."

She passed him the burnt marshmallow and took another for herself. The Chela uncorked the wine with a corkscrew attached to his Swiss Army knife.

Matty looked at him. "Why did you come here?" She took a sip of the wine and cut a piece of cheese.

The Chela grinned, slipping into the lotus position. "I'm getting to that part," he said. "I just wanted you to be comfortable."

Matty nodded. She was comfortable, she was relaxed. Toasted marshmallows were a childhood favourite.

"There I was in Toronto, having dinner in a Chinese restaurant. It was Friday. The Beefys ate fish on Friday and I can't stand the stuff so I always went out that night. This was six years after I'd left Hot Stuff at the border. There he was in Toronto, having dinner in the same Chinese restaurant."

Rasputin was with him. Rasputin had shot a policeman and was keeping a low profile. He and Hot Stuff were living on a farm while they were waiting to pull a robbery. Reptile was out west looking for land. Reptile had gone straight which is what Rasputin intended to do once he had the money.

One strong feeling ran through them all: a hatred of the law. Rasputin saw a friend in every criminal; to Hot Stuff a heroic deed meant any act of defiance. They listened eagerly to the Chela's account of the Beefys. The three shared a deep contempt for law-abiding citizens.

The Beefys had been good to him, said the Chela, and better still they trusted him. Their safe contained enough money to buy freedom for all of them. He could arrange a break-in and never be suspected. Hot Stuff paid for a round of drinks and said now they were really talking.

A week later Rasputin cracked the Beefys' safe. The Chela let him in through the backdoor during the middle of the night when everyone was sleeping. But the Chela had made a miscalculation. The safe contained less than twenty-five thousand dollars.

The Chela stayed on with the Beefys until things quietened down. Hot Stuff and Rasputin went west to join Reptile; they'd heard he was living with a commune in the Kootenays. When it came time for the Chela to leave, the Beefys resigned themselves to sadness. Mrs. Beefy prepared a last supper – a smoked picnic ham studded with cloves and covered with a brown sugar glaze and tinned pineapple wedges. Beefy choked on a clove and was rushed from the table, blubbering. Later in the evening Mr. Beefy took a photograph of his wife sitting on the prune-coloured divan, an arm around each of her boys.

The Chela took a Greyhound across the prairies as far as Edmonton. From Edmonton he hitched a ride through the Rockies, got off in Nelson where a farm vehicle took him right to the gates of Brother Life-Is-Real's commune. The farmer warned him that there were loose women inside, women walking around stark raving naked in the middle of winter. Free love, too, for those who wanted to pay the price.

The Big House was not visible from the road. The Chela stashed his suitcase behind a stump and started walking. The long journey had left him burned out and exhausted. The farmer's running commentary had done nothing to allay his doubts.

A dog came trotting down the road towards him and stopped in its tracks. Behind the dog drifted a tall willowy youth wearing an Indian bedspread. The Chela stepped forward and introduced himself. The youth smiled and scribbled him a note. *"I am sorry. I cannot speak to you. I have taken a ninety-nine-year lease on silence."*

The Chela went to the Big House where he found his friends. Rasputin, his face the colour of a hothouse tomato, was standing on his head. He explained that he was taking the cosmic overview. They'd told him he was uptight when he skipped the Creative Aggression class.

Round the walls were hung photographs of friends from previous incarnations. Above the fireplace was a photo of Life-Is-Real himself. He had tie-dyed hair, the Chela told Matty, and made Vesuvius look like an iceberg. Rasputin had to pay him so he didn't go squealing to the cops.

"The cops were looking for us," said the Chela, pouring more wine. "They wanted to ask us some questions. I guess the Beefys had figured it out. I'm glad I never left them a forwarding address."

The Chela asked Hot Stuff where the women were. The only person he'd seen, besides his friends, looked like a eunuch.

Hot Stuff roared with laughter. The youth was the resident sex-therapist. If they stayed on at the commune they made a ninety-nine-year vow of chastity. Then, if they survived, they took a ninety-nine-year lease on silence and after that they graduated with a one-way ticket to Nirvana.

"Life-Is-Real, however, was more down-to-earth. He had two women to himself every night, one to clean his toenails and the other – if you'll pardon the language – to suck his cock. I told Reptile to start packing immediately. I'd had my consciousness raised about as far as it would go."

The Chela suggested they start their own commune farther north out in the bush where the long arm of the law rarely set foot. He proposed a real Human Workshop of men and women working side by side without depending on the rest of the world for anything. The women would cook, care for the gardens, make love, have babies. The men would hunt, clear land, make love, have a good time.

Rasputin asked him where would they get the women. The Chela told him God would provide.

Within hours they were on their way. They took Hot Stuff's van, a beat-up Volkswagen with 155,000 miles on the engine. It had been on its last legs, Hot Stuff warned them, ever since it learned to stand up. They drove north and west until the engine blew up; they pushed the van into a ditch under the sign saying WELCOME TO ONANUGA.

They headed for the Land Registry Office. The Chela waited outside, being the most conspicuous, while the others studied maps of the area. Rasputin wanted to go north, as far as the river would take them. Everyone agreed and they rented a boat from a fisherman.

Six days and many arguments later they reached Squinskut. They stole a canoe, abandoning their battered rental. Reptile navigated from that point on while Rasputin and Hot Stuff paddled. The Chela lay in the bow of the canoe, reading aloud from the Bible.

"I'd gotten interested in religion when I was staying at the Beefys. I even took a Bible postal course. It was supposed to give my life a whole new meaning.

"Well, then I saw *The Bible*–one of those movie spectaculars. It really got me thinking. Since I'd seen the movie I decided to read the book. I guess it pointed me in the right direction."

In three weeks time they had reached the rapids. Reptile discovered the trail leading inland, the old blaze marks forming pitch-ringed scars on the tree trunks. They followed the trail as far as the trapper's cabin where the Chela revised his plan for his self-sufficient colony.

Hot Stuff and Rasputin were impatient; they wanted women, and God was taking his time. They returned to the south with Reptile to recruit members. The Chela stayed alone, getting to know the land.

It was about this time he first started having visions. He was sitting in the outhouse one morning, meditating on the trees, when he saw an image–a woman hanging in the sky and gesturing to him with her hand. He got up and followed her out onto the muskeg.

She came down out of the air and sat on a stump–the Chela said he'd carved a compass there later so he'd remember the exact spot. She asked him if he'd like to have a picnic, and before he could answer she reached inside her cloak and brought out a couple of bottles of beer. Imported beer, too, he told Matty.

The woman had a white light all around her head, but she kept her face hidden. They drank the beer together–she didn't mention food but the Chela was too stunned to think about it until afterwards–and then she disappeared.

The next day she returned, and the day after that. She would always bring him something–a tin of smoked oysters, a jar of marmalade–she seemed to know what he liked. After a while he started taking her for granted and then she didn't come as often. The last time he saw her she told him about the Messiah.

She said, "The Coming King will physically return to earth a second time. To Ephratah will come a Chosen Woman, and she will nurture him"–or words to that effect. Then she disappeared leaving a pound of cooking chocolate. The Chela never saw her again.

From then on he ate berries and whatever he was able to trap. In the middle of June his men returned, bringing with them a woman.

At first the Chela thought it was the woman of his vision, returning to visit in an earthly form. Then he thought it was the Chosen Woman of whom the vision had spoken.

She was neither one. Rasputin and the others had gone back to Brother Life's hoping to persuade some of the women there to come away with them to the wilderness. Briony Mark, chairperson of the Vegetarian Feminists Collective in San Francisco was in Nelson crusading for female and animal rights. Her women were looking for a new life, she told members of the Naturopathic Association, one where it was possible to live and eat both pleasantly and humanely. Reptile told her about the Chela, how he was looking for a similar arrangement, and Briony, without any persuasion, agreed to a meeting.

The long journey did not discourage her. When the Chela saw her striding across the clearing, his men shuffling behind like so many sheep, he knew what they were up against. For two days and two nights he discussed his plans with Briony and for the rest of the week she discussed hers with him. Finally they reached an agreement; Hot Stuff was called in to witness the contract.

Briony knew there were certain advantages to having men around; the Chela knew that no community could be self-sufficient without women. Briony, however, was a devout vegetarian; she wanted a separate colony for her women where they would not be exposed to the meat-eating men.

Their roles were clearly defined in the contract: Briony wanted houses built to her own specifications, she also wanted supplies, things they couldn't grow themselves; the Chela wanted children. If they were to establish any real foundation to their new life they would have to allow for future generations. Briony agreed, and drew up a plan for the Pregnancy Wishes Rituals.

Once a month the Chela would visit the women's commune. The other men would not have the same privileges – it would lower the standards. The Chela conferred with his men and they agreed, laughingly. Rules were only made, said Rasputin, to give others the pleasure of breaking them.

The Chela told Briony about the new Messiah, how the King would be born of a Chosen Woman. She could care for him until he was six months old, at which time the boy would be delivered to the Chela. If the babies were girls they could remain at Ephratah. Briony thought it was a fair exchange.

She returned to California to discuss the colony with her women. All summer the four men worked on the cabins, building a small community. Briony had asked for twelve separate living quarters, a Communal Hall and half a dozen outbuildings. The men worked from dawn to dusk felling trees, cutting cedar bolts, splitting shakes and making planks. Hot Stuff had constructed a saw mill from an old truck engine whose pieces he had dragged in from the river, one at a time.

With autumn approaching, the Chela began to grow restless. He worried that Briony wouldn't come back, that she'd reveal his plans to the whole world instead.

The Chela needed more men; he sent Rasputin south where he stayed for two months. In October when he returned he had with him more than fifty men. Draft-dodgers, hippies, school dropouts, would-be homesteaders, junkies, small-time gangsters, juvenile delinquents: "At one time," said the Chela, "those bunkhouses were full. Now there's just seven of us. We're all that's left."

Briony had returned a month later, and her women had come with her. The men set to work on another group of buildings–their own settlement–further north again and nearer the lake. The Chela paid monthly visits to Ephratah though he was never actually seen by any of the women. Briony had them convinced that he was some kind of deity, and she didn't want him to spoil the image.

The first winter was hard; both communes suffered from the brutal living conditions. Many people took sick; most of the livestock died. At the end of May when there was still snow in place, the ground was not ready for planting.

There was no money left from the Beefys' safe. Briony needed grain. A long-time admirer of John Noyes, founder of the Oneida Community in the eastern United States–a vegetarian sect who, while forbidding even the wearing of leather and wool, obtained their primary source of income by trapping animals for furs–Briony decided that her own women would become trappers. She didn't expect to operate on such a grand scale as Noyes and his followers, whose annual sales from furs, by 1864, amounted to $100,000 with the manufacture of more than 300,000 pelts, but even a hundred pelts a year would give them financial independence. The Manger was fixed up to accommodate the pelts; Rasputin and Hot Stuff, who'd had no experience in trapping, willingly volunteered their services.

By early December they were in full operation. Briony took the first load of pelts south, and with the pelts sold and food in the Barn, Celandine's first baby was born.

"A boy," said the Chela, pausing to poke the coals, "a monster like Beefy. He died the next day. It was Christmas."

24

It was Reptile's idea to make charcoal. They'd spent two winters hacking down trees in order to keep warm; if they spent two months every summer making charcoal they could lie back and relax for the rest of the year. They would also need charcoal if they wanted to make gunpowder. Alder and willow were the best woods to use, and these were both in plentiful supply.

Hot Stuff was enthusiastic. Rasputin opposed the plan on practical grounds. They were living in a forest with enough wood to last forever. He didn't see the point in making charcoal.

There was little work involved, Reptile insisted. Charcoal was more efficient than wood and had twice the heating power.

The Chela was concerned that the wood was too green. They'd had difficulty burning it in their stoves because it hadn't been seasoned properly.

Hot Stuff had come from a long line of charcoal burners. "There's nothing that won't burn," he said, "if you know how to burn it." As a boy he'd helped his father preparing land to plant turnips. "My father, he could burn anything. Tins, compost, vermin."

The Chela agreed to the plan; Hot Stuff helped Reptile build a test pit while the others looked on, grudgingly. "Hot

Stuff and Reptile, they see things differently," the Chela told Matty. "Charcoal burning's no fun unless you happen to enjoy it. To most people it's just work, plain and dirty. They don't like the heat. They don't like breathing charcoal dust in their lungs."

The Chela added more charcoal to the fire. "At first we only burned wood," he said, "but then Reptile started experimenting. Vegetable peelings, corn-cobs, rice hulks, nut shells, fruit seeds. It was a real fight to get Briony to part with her compost.

"Then we had an accident–a fire in one of the bunkhouses. A real waste of bodies. Nothing but ash."

Shortly afterwards, Celandine's baby died. Hot Stuff suggested they make use of the corpse–there'd been too much waste already. Bones, he said, could be used to make charcoal, but only if the burning was properly regulated.

A kiln was built for Celandine's baby. The tiny body caused uneven carbonization in the pit and the resulting charcoal was inferior in quality. When Valerian's baby died, Reptile rectified the situation. He burned only the bones, together with wood of the same density.

"We're still learning," said the Chela, after a pause. He picked up a piece of charcoal and handed it to Matty. It was weightless, yet every knot and grain was preserved. It was as if a ghost had passed through the wood, light and metallic in touch and sound, leaving behind its shadow.

"Charcoal is a beautiful thing to turn out," said the Chela, "when your kiln is burnt and opened up. It's like opening a grave and finding a ghost inside."

Matty waited until the Chela was asleep. Then she put on the moccasins he'd given her, and Christian's green jacket. She was still diapered under her blood-stained trousers but she didn't have time to deal with that problem. She only knew that she wanted to get away. She'd walk in circles, sleep in the cold, starve, eat roots, face bears – anything to be delivered from this madman.

The sky was clear but there was no moon. She stepped out of the hut, shivering, and drew the jacket around her. The Chela had given it to her – as a keepsake perhaps? She wished Christian were inside it with her. He would show her the way.

The path led past the cookhouse. The wrong way, she realized: there was a lamp burning in the window and she imagined she could hear a hack-saw cutting away in the dark. Bodies being chopped up for Hot Stuff's Crematorium. Eyes, ears, tongues, tiny hearts – everything sorted according to density. But the Chela said they burned only the bones. What, then, did they do with the bodies?

She stood still for a moment; she hadn't avoided the puddles and her feet were already soaking. She might as well be hamstrung for all the use moccasins were. The sawing had stopped and the air was thick with silence. The whole world held its breath for her in darkness.

She thought of removing the moccasins, but she'd be worse off without them. She took another step forward, stumbling over a pile of hides. She lay where she had fallen, with something sharp poking into her ribs. She dared not move, like a carnival girl in a blade box: if she moved something would pierce her, and a hundred gawking people would give money to see her blood.

No one came. There *was* no one. She realized after a while that her body stank of dead animal, that the hides she was lying in were recent ones and hadn't been properly treated. She forced herself to get up and made her way – the hides were moulting and she was covered in hair – past the cookhouse window.

She followed the path that skirted the bunkhouses. Beyond them was safety, the trail to the kiln and after that the muskeg. She would make it there by daylight, in spite of the moccasins. When she reached the compass marker she'd turn east and head for the river.

"Going somewhere?"

He was standing in her path. From the smell, if Tansy's description had been accurate, it was Rasputin. He was breathing irregularly as if he'd come from a great distance to stop her. Matty was sure her legs would sag under her.

She wasn't going anywhere. "For a walk," she said, "to the kiln – and back."

She wished she hadn't added *and back*. It didn't sound convincing.

"So late?"

He was all around her, like darkness, drinking her in. She avoided his eyes; Tansy said his pupils were like a hypnotized rabbit's. If he forced you to look at them you would disappear into the dark. Down into a rabbit hole where there was no backing out.

"You alone?"

He knew she was. He knew she was running – from the Chela, from the lot of them. She had no desire to be made into charcoal. No matter how beautiful she'd look, no matter how well turned out.

Rasputin took her arm. Her arms and legs were numb; the weakness was centred in her stomach and chest.

She felt as if she were floating, weightless as charcoal, a soft thing in Rasputin's hands. He was taking her to one of the bunkhouses, pulling her up the steps. He kicked open the door and pushed her inside ahead of him.

Three men were slouched over a table, playing cards and arguing. One of them looked up, saw Matty, and nudged his partner.

"I brought you something to play with," said Rasputin. "She was taking a walk – by herself – in the dark. I didn't think it was proper. This ain't exactly a good neighbourhood."

Black Sam, lost in the shadows of the dimly lit room, snorted. Crow Bait flashed the peace sign. "None of us are safe," he said, quailing under Rasputin's glare. "I mean like they're looking for us, right? That's their trip, man, like I mean it's not *my* trip but I can dig the trip they're into okay? Know what I'm talking about? I mean this dude puts a gun to my head, okay well that's really far-out, I can dig it. He's a beautiful human being, he's just scared so he can't be free and love everybody. We all get scared, man, I mean nobody's different."

Rasputin spat across the table onto the stove. The spit-ball sizzled and danced, growing smaller and smaller until finally there was silence in the room.

He pushed Matty into a chair and tied her hands behind her. The three men carried on with their game, glancing nervously over their shoulders from time to time at Rasputin.

"Here," said Rasputin, forcing a bottle between Matty's lips. "Have a shot of Hot Stuff's whisky. Tonight it's on the house."

Matty spat the whisky on the floor. She closed her eyes tight, flinching at the blow she anticipated. She blinked. Nothing happened.

"I say kill the bastards," said General Electric, continuing the argument Rasputin had interrupted, "before they kill us. Start with the politicians – they're the most corrupt. Let them know we mean serious business."

Black Sam threw in his hand, snorting. Crow Bait squealed. The General with his freshly mown head bristling like a toilet brush, grunted. They reminded Matty of three little pigs.

She remembered a strange tale her father had told her, about a man who concealed his children in a disused oven because he was afraid of the mysterious power of the Christ child.

"What have you got in that oven?" asked the Divine young visitor.

"Pigs," replied the father.

"Pigs they be!" declared the Christ child. And when the oven was opened, out rushed three little pigs.

The tale had a moral – her father's stories always had

morals. The children were turned into swine because they mocked the boy Jesus. She could use his help at the moment if he would return to earth, physically. He could change the three men into card-playing pigs.

She dismissed the image instantly. Pigs, she realized, would eat anything. Human beings, above all, they considered a delicacy.

"We could sell their bones as souvenirs," the General continued. "Crow Bait, you'd be the distributor. We could sell them to tourists. *Genuine Carbonized Politician's Thighbone.* Hand-picked by local terrorists."

"Hey, man," said Crow Bait, "I mean this is getting heavy."

"Where from do you intend on getting the bones?" asked Black Sam, sniffing instead of snorting.

"Wake up, Sam. From the bodies, where else? But listen to this: *Made in Canada, this unique and hand-crafted collector's item. A must for your mantle. In Bone-Black or Ash-White.* C.B., you know how to spell. You're in charge of advertising."

"I got another idea," cried Crow Bait. *"Real, genuine conversation piece."*

"You don't say *real genuine*," the General interrupted. "It can't be genuine unless it *is* real."

"He don't know shit from Grade Eight," said Sam.

"What are you talking about?" said Rasputin, to all of them.

"We're going to start a revolution," said the General, "with or without assistance from the Chela. We're tired of sitting here making gunpowder for nothing. You, for instance, Crow Bait. You could become famous."

"I could get into that," Crow Bait nodded.

"Sure, sure," said Rasputin, "you all know what you're doing. If you play your cards right, C.B., you might be the next Mr. President. The General here can organize your army. You got to think big, eh, General?"

Crow Bait looked at his cards, shaking his head in disbelief.

"That sounds like a heavy power-trip, man. I mean, like the *President*!"

Black Sam shuffled the deck. "What's the matter with you, boy? Long's you play your cards right ain't nobody gonna assassinate you."

Crow Bait looked at his cards and then looked helplessly at the General. The General was not a nigger-lover, though being from the South he'd had to put up with them most of his life.

"This ain't no game," he said, mimicking Black Sam's accent. His eyes narrowed as Sam's grew bigger. "C.B. don't have to take no shit. Not from nobody he don't."

"You talk like a nigger, boy," Sam said, imitating the General who was, after all, not a good mimic. The General leapt to his feet and pulled a knife. Crow Bait fled squawking into the night.

Sam lunged for the whisky bottle and smashed it on the edge of the table. Then, baring his arm, he slashed from his wrist to his elbow. A dark ribbon of blood coiled onto the whisky-stained floor.

"Match that, honkey!" he hissed. "Let's see what kind of guts *you* got!"

Before the General had time to react, Rasputin kicked the knife from his surprised hand and sent him flying headfirst through the open door. The bleeding Sam was sent after him in a similar fashion. Rasputin wiped his hands on his jacket, sat down and opened another bottle.

"If they want to fight," he said, "they can fight out there like the animals."

Matty would not look at him. The cords sawed at her wrists, cutting off circulation; she tried to wriggle free but realized it was useless. Even if she did get loose, she wouldn't get very far. Rasputin was not watching her but she had the feeling he saw everything.

An hour later, when the whisky was nearly all gone, he untied her from the chair. He put the rope around her neck – she half-expected to be blindfolded, at least offered a last cigarette – and pulled her out into the dark. If she struggled to escape, the knot would pull tight and choke her.

He took her to another of the bunkhouses, unlocked the door and pushed her inside. She heard the padlock snapping into place, and footsteps receding into the night.

She undid the rope and lifted it over her head. Her teeth were chattering with cold and fright. She was standing in a dormitory that looked like the inside of a slave-ship. Long lines of bunk beds had been pushed against the walls, and in the middle of the room there was a pile of old mattresses. Stuffing oozed from their seams like little clouds of pus.

On top of the mattresses there was a pile of rusty bedsprings. The floor was littered with garbage – mouldy clothing, scraps of metal, empty bottles and tins, old newspapers. She thought perhaps they were saving it to be burned in a future kiln. The Chela had said that Reptile was fond of experimenting.

Between the door and the wall she could see a slit of light. There were no windows in the shed, but she guessed it was almost morning. She collected some newspapers and made herself a bed. She was exhausted, she could tell, but she didn't intend to sleep.

A scrap of paper lay between her bed and the door. The bold red lettering caught her eye and she reached to pick it up.

R's the butcher, S likes rare meat,
General Electric corns the beef.

Matty heard footsteps returning. She quickly tucked the note into her trousers.

25

Matty was banished from the Chela's cabin; from now on she was to stay alone at night locked inside the dormitory with the garbage and the rotting mattresses. Lying awake on her bed of newspapers, Christian's green jacket her only comfort, she pictured the mattresses as they once must have been, the bodies they would have supported, bodies like her own weakened by a diet of rice – occasionally flavoured with bits of deer offal – and gravy, bodies covered with half-healed sores, bodies no longer resembling bodies, but destined – for what she didn't know, nor for what reason. She would rather have stayed drugged on Valerian's potions, stayed married to Dan in the womb of East Oyster. She should have married a dentist, should have given him children. *A person without destiny was not bound by the inescapable.*

The Chela refused to see her; he regarded her attempted escape as a personal insult. He had, after all, trusted her. He had given her his house, his hospitality, his life history.

As further punishment, she was made to work in the cookhouse. She was to help Rasputin prepare meals for the men. Rasputin spent most of his time in the kitchen butchering. The room stank of blood and meat; Rasputin stank of blood, meat, and charcoal.

But his presence kept her awake. His body emanated an electrical power, and though he seemed hardly conscious of her most of the time, it helped her to recharge when her mind went half-asleep into some uneasy dream or other. When he did look at her – she had still managed to avoid direct eye-contact – she felt as though she had been struck right through her sexual centre, and her sexual centre happened to move according to where his eyes touched. Sexual intercourse, she'd read, was a lowbrow way of forgetting oneself: right now all she wanted was to be somebody else, and for this reason she grew wary of him.

Rasputin had a collection of skulls. He kept them on a skull-rack over the counter where he butchered. They were human skulls, painted with human blood he told Matty. Some were tattooed, decorated with beads and bits of glass; others had stones for eyes, pierced noses. One of them had hair, long, black, and braided.

"It started out real innocent," he said to her one morning when she was chopping onions for one of his greasy stews. Rasputin was slicing liver and blood oozed from a dirty rag that was wrapped around his little finger. Occasionally he removed the rag and sucked at the open wound.

"We were in it for the money. We used to shrink the heads – it was easier to pack them out that way – and sell them for a fortune. I got tired of the work and kind of retired early. I'm still collecting, but I like to keep them natural."

He grinned and looked up at the row of skulls. "These here are the survivors. Only trouble is they look too damn human. When you shrink a head, you know, it gets a new personality."

Onions made her cry: she'd forgotten that. She began to make thicker slices, imagining the onion was Rasputin's head.

He dropped a potato into the broth. "I guess you've figured it out, eh. We do eat people around here. It was getting kind of wasteful – I mean taking the heads and leaving the rest – so we cooked up a bunch of our own recipes. Why do you think Stan brought you here in the first place?"

Matty continued slicing. The cheeks were difficult. It was hard to get a grip on them.

"A lot of people are pretty tough, especially the types who end up here. There was this one old dude a few years back, for instance. A prospector. Tough as his boots, he was. I made a whole mess of jerky out of that one!

"But take someone like yourself, you're mostly vegetable. You'd be nice and tender. We have to fatten you up a bit, get you to relax. If you kill something when it's scared, the meat's stringy."

He paused and she could feel his eyes again, like hot stones imbedding themselves in her skin. She added the onions to the bubbling pot on the stove. The water was covered with yellow scum.

"It's your turn soon," said Rasputin, "they'll be starting on your kiln." He studied her head, parting the hair straight down from the crown to the base of her scalp, and slitting the skin with his eyes. She could feel her parting line, the skin being turned back on both sides and being slipped from her skull like a stocking from a foot. She felt her head shrinking to the size of a large orange. An exact miniature of her former self, she would be his trophy.

Hot Stuff was sitting on the steps of his bunkhouse complaining about the quality of the marmalade when Matty approached him one morning. She was allowed to visit the kilns as long as someone went with her, and Hot Stuff said he was going to join Reptile after breakfast. They were setting a new pit.

Rasputin had driven her from the bunkhouse with an obscene threat.

"Best leave him alone for a while," said Hot Stuff. "It's his mean streak acting up. He gets like this when the weather's on the change. Stay out of his way and he'll forget you."

Reptile was preparing a load of pine. "Top bits are punky,"

he said, as Matty and Hot Stuff came into the clearing. He flicked the loose rot away with his finger. "Look," he said, disgustedly, "sawdust!"

"You've got shit for brains," said Hot Stuff. "I thought you were supposed to be the genius! You stacked that wood yourself, remember? You should have known it would turn out punky!"

Reptile looked at him smugly. "I said the *top* bits are punky. It's one hundred per cent underneath."

He'd cut the wood the previous summer and stacked it to dry in the open air. The larger pieces he'd split and trimmed straight while the crooked and bent branches he'd cut into smaller lengths and stacked separately.

Crow Bait strolled into the clearing. "It's like a beautiful day, man," he said, taking a deep breath. "I'm really tripping out on it, I mean like *already.*" He pulled a bag from his pocket and began rolling himself a joint.

Reptile had set to work building his mound. He'd chosen level, well-drained ground relatively sheltered from the wind.

"The best size for a kiln is from six to eight feet in height and thirteen to twenty feet in diameter," he said, looking at Matty, "so I make mine approximately seven feet high and eighteen feet in diameter. That gives us nearly eight and a half to eight and three-quarters – it's closer to eight and a half actually – cords of wood. A cord, as you know, is a hundred and twenty-eight cubic feet, piled, or roughly sixty-four cubic feet solid of cordwood."

Matty nodded. Her knowledge of charcoal burning had been limited to her high-school studies, to whatever she'd managed to cram before writing her finals. *During the Middle Ages charcoal burning caused much of the deforestation of the densely populated European continent. For centuries charcoal was the only fuel used in metal smelting, and in order to obtain it in sufficient quantities immense English forests were destroyed.*

Hot Stuff had prepared the site by burning slash all winter. Crow Bait, determined to construct a pit of his own, had chosen to build next to them, in a muddy depression.

"I wish you'd approach things more scientifically," said Reptile. "I told you before–that ground's too wet."

"Right on," said Crow Bait, offering Matty a toke. She refused the joint and Crow Bait exhaled a disapproving "far-out."

Matty watched as Reptile laid three billets, ends overlapping, on top of the mound. The billets formed a small triangle. The centre of the hearth was always built on a mound. It increased the draught and provided drainage for any liquid produced.

"It's like building a log cabin," he said, "or a card house. What you end up with depends on your foundations."

He laid three more billets on the first lot, repeating the process until the logs formed a triangular chimney about six feet high. He set more logs, vertically, leaning against the chimney in successive rings.

Matty expected the construction to collapse. But Reptile worked patiently, setting each log in place and making the kiln as symmetrical as possible. Crow Bait's kiln, set in the depression, looked angular and lop-sided while Reptile's was flat on top and sloped away evenly on every side.

To exclude all air, other than, as he explained, a minimum amount necessary for carbonization, Reptile made an inner and outer covering. The inner layer consisted of strips of earth cut from the muskeg. The sods were placed grass-downwards and soaked thoroughly with water. The outer covering was a mixture of damp earth, charcoal dust, dead leaves and moss. The top of the flue was left open.

The pit was ready for burning. Crow Bait had quit hours ago, the sun was setting, and the men were getting hungry. Neither Hot Stuff nor Reptile had stopped for lunch and Reptile had been working since he got up in the morning.

Matty left them patting down the outer covering with the backs of their shovels. Reluctantly she returned to the cookhouse.

The following day was bright and windy. Reptile was up long before the others making a cedar-bough screen on the windward side of his pit. Matty went to watch when Hot Stuff had finished his breakfast. Crow Bait struggled down halfway through the morning.

Crow Bait didn't think it was windy. He wasn't going to build a screen in any case. He didn't care whether his pit burned too quickly.

Reptile had a charcoal fire burning a few feet from the kiln. Hot Stuff shovelled the red-hot pieces down the flue. The glowing coals ignited the dry billets at the bottom of the heap. When the fire caught, Hot Stuff filled the flue with kindling.

Reptile passed him a wooden pole. "Shove it down with this," he said, as Hot Stuff added another armload of kindling. "As the flue fills up it gets red hot," he said, turning to Matty. "I wouldn't be able to give you an exact temperature offhand, but I'll figure it out for you later if you're still interested."

Crow Bait was frying wood-bugs on the end of a joint. Matty was not interested, she was too tired to be interested in anything. She'd been awake most of the night trying to think of a new escape plan. Reptile covered the flue with a heavy frying pan and told her it would have to be removed periodically so they could feed in more wood.

The day dragged on. Hot Stuff and Reptile were engrossed in their work. Crow Bait abandoned his kiln for a tab of acid. Hot Stuff wanted to know where it came from and Crow Bait told him Switzerland. "It's Grey Barrel, man. You know, like *Grey Barrel.*"

At suppertime Reptile removed the frying pan and covered the hole with a chunk of damp turf.

"The next part's the hardest," he said, wiping the sweat from his forehead with the back of his hand. "Once the pit is closed you've got to go by the colour of the smoke. You have to watch it carefully until the charcoal is done–anywhere from four days to a week, depending on the weather. Up here it burns fast. In hot places the burning's slower."

Matty did not want to go back to the cookhouse. Reptile went for her–he'd been summoned by the Chela–and returned a while later with two pieces of steak. He also brought word that the Chela was going to Ephratah.

He didn't bring any food for Matty; if she wanted her rice and gravy, Rasputin said she'd have to ask him for it. She'd ignored him the night before when he'd slipped his bloody cleaver between her legs, had managed not to flinch but had gone on stir-frying the rice. Tonight she was too tired to keep up her guard. Reptile offered her a piece of his steak but she told him she wasn't hungry.

The news of the Chela's departure shed a new light on her plan. The trail to the muskeg would be closely guarded for the next four or five days while Reptile and Hot Stuff kept a twenty-four-hour watch over the kiln, so that route was out of the question. The only other way left open to her was the trail leading past the Chela's. She hadn't considered it seriously before, but with him out of the way the only obstacle left was the cookhouse.

Hot Stuff took the first shift and Matty sat up talking to him. Reptile would relieve him at midnight. Meanwhile he was sleeping in a nearby shelter.

"I was raised like this so I'm used to it," Hot Stuff said to her. "My family's been charcoal burners as far back as anyone can remember. I'm really the one who got Reptile interested. I taught him everything he's ever going to know, but Stan, he never gives people credit."

She had to escape. The idea was to keep Hot Stuff talking. At midnight he'd go to sleep and she would stay on talking to Reptile. Reptile trusted her, she could tell. He'd let her walk back to the dormitory by herself.

Hot Stuff told her he'd spent his early life in England. His family made their camps in the Forest of Dean or else on one of the big estates, burning two or three kilns a year to supply the charcoal to the kitchens for roasting game. When an area was denuded, they moved on.

Charcoal burners were treated like gypsies, only worse; people knew they were too proud to beg. Hot Stuff's father, Purkiss Strutt, named after the charcoal burner Purkiss who, over nine hundred years ago, removed the body of King William to Winchester on his cart, looked and smelled like a troglodyte after so many years of stooping at the pits. "That's where I got the hump," said Hot Stuff, pointing over his shoulder. "It runs in the family – from a long way back."

The family lived in a hut slightly more modern than those built by Stone Age man. The hut had a pole frame, was lined with coarse sacking and covered with twigs and sections of turf. "You've seen Stan's shack? Well, I designed that. He probably told you different, of course. I'll tell you one thing – he built it himself. That's why it's so goddamn flimsy!"

Hot Stuff was the youngest of ten children. In the heart of winter all thirteen of them – Purkiss and his wife Mary, and old grandad Lothar plus the children – left the hut and bundled into a rickety caravan for warmth. It was even more crowded inside the caravan, and Hot Stuff and his brother Frank took turns sleeping on top of one another. On Sundays they changed out of their rags and went into town to sing with the Salvation Army.

Hot Stuff was still a boy when the war started. The family moved north to set up another camp; his father made them a shelter in a discarded truck body.

Charcoal burning was becoming an industry. Charcoal was used in the manufacture of synthetic silk for parachutes, in bulk explosives for blasting and in making filters for anti-gas respirators. Not that Purkiss and his family were aware of any of these facts. They simply tended their pits as they'd always done, let the heap burn, raked away the ashes and covered the remaining charcoal with fresh earth to let it cool. After two or three days they packed it into sacks, and men came from town to transport it to the factories.

After the war Purkiss worked alongside lumberjacks from Canada. There was a small logging industry in Scotland that extended down over the border and out towards the west. Where the Ministry of Supply had cleared areas of forest for natural timber, they encouraged the manufacture of charcoal on more modern lines. Purkiss was not happy working with the large new iron kilns, and after the first year he emigrated to Canada. He'd been given some land in the wilds of Nova Scotia. Purkiss dedicated the rest of his life to clearing the land and raising turnips.

Hot Stuff took off his cap and scratched his bald spot. He always wore the same cap, he told her, when he was burning. It had flaps to keep his ears from getting hot and a badge on the front showing a beaver eating a maple leaf. CANADA, it said.

"I left home when I was sixteen," he continued, "and hitchhiked around. I met up with these gypsies. They taught me fortune-telling and how to con people out of their money. I went on a thieving binge with them, right across the country. One of them was a firebreather–him and me we became buddies.

"One night we were walking around. We'd robbed a cigarette machine and I had five bucks in my pocket. We decided to live it up–you know, rent a hotel room. I'd been toying with the idea of becoming a firebreather myself but up until then I'd had no real experience. So when my buddy stepped out to get us some more booze, what I did was I took a drink of gasoline. I held it in my mouth and tried to spit it into my lighter. The whole thing exploded–blew up in my face.

"So the hotel's on fire. I'm on fire, too, but all I can think of is where did I put that five bucks because without it I have no money to pay for the room. Turned out it didn't matter. There was no room left to pay for, anyway.

"I landed up in hospital. My buddy came to see me a few times. He's the one who gave me my name. He gave me this cap, too, when I lost the hand."

He saw her staring and drew the stump inside his sleeve. He stood up, stretching. Reptile had come down to join them by the fire. Hot Stuff said he'd take her back to the dormitory, but Matty said she wasn't sleepy. Hot Stuff told Reptile to keep a close eye on her, to make sure she didn't try to do anything funny.

It wasn't hard to keep Reptile talking, though Matty had more difficulty keeping awake listening to him. He explained why the kiln needed their constant attention: it had to do with the regulation of the burning.

The method of regulation was to make vent holes to increase the draught and expedite burning, and to close vent holes and water the covering to retard burning. Vent holes were usually made on the second day, on the sheltered side of the kiln at about two thirds its height. As the burning proceeded the holes were covered and others made lower down, each series of holes being covered in turn until the base was reached and carbonization completed.

"As the temperature rises and the moisture in the wood turns to steam, there's a danger of an explosion," he said. "The cover has to fit properly, has to be porous enough to let the steam out but not so porous as to let in too much air."

Matty said she really should be going. She didn't think Reptile ought to leave the kiln; if anything went wrong she would feel responsible. Reptile agreed. If she went straight to her room, he said, she could go without an escort.

Her room. The thought made her shudder. She wouldn't be going back there again, ever. The rats could have it, and the lice, and the beetles.

She said goodnight to Reptile and left him worrying about his vents. Hurrying through the darkness she had only one thought: to make it past the bunkhouses, past the cookhouse where Rasputin would be sleeping.

There was no light burning in the cookhouse window. She imagined him snoring, lying fully clothed on his sweaty mattress. She imagined him dead, lying disembowelled and decapitated, flies circling his still-open eyes as she peered down into them and saw nothing but her own reflection.

The moon cast a cold light onto the boughs of a silver birch; everything seemed to shimmer and Matty felt as if she were part of some shivering ghost-world. She could see in the darkness as clearly as if it were daylight.

She crept away from the cookhouse, out into the night. She felt as if she were gliding; she was aware of an unusual lightness. Insects and moonbeams seemed to pass right through her. *Like a spirit, Dan said, you make yourself invisible.*

"You're late."

The voice, the foul smell. The thick shadow. Heavy breathing.

She had almost reached the Chela's. Rasputin had not been sleeping after all. He'd been lying in wait for her.

He lit a match and held it up to her face. He stood squarely in front of her, transfixing her with his eyes.

The match went out. She turned away, quickly, but his eyes picked her out of the dark. She felt his hand on her chin, forcing her to look straight ahead. His hand was hurting her, diffusing pain throughout the whole of her body.

He struck another match. She felt paralyzed. She tried to speak but her mouth wouldn't open. The words stuck in her throat like tiny splinters of glass.

His black eyes shone, phosphorescent. From the centre of his pupils came two rays of light. She was drawn to the light like an animal; her instinct told her that the light meant danger. She couldn't move, in any case. His eyes had numbed her, punctured her senses.

The light-rays flowed into one another, merged into a mandala–a glowing circle concentrated on a fixed point behind her eyes. It moved towards her, then moved away again. When it approached she could see his eyes, burning through the centre of the circle, but then the circle would recede back into his skull, and his eyes would vanish, dragging her own with them.

She was aware of him speaking. She thought he said, *I was expecting you earlier*, but she stood motionless, unable to reply.

She didn't like pain, no. He would hurt her, hang her on a meat hook. He'd said he would do that if she came to the kitchen late.

She watched his eyes flicker. He was thinking about her naked. Tied up, helpless, cut into pieces. Thirteen red bundles: a butcher's dozen. He was stroking her throat with his bloody cleaver. He was sucking her blood and making it into sausages.

She was not going to be frightened. She was not going to show him that she was frightened.

He was lighting a cigarette. Butting it on her nipples. He was drawing circles around her breasts in charcoal. Two hearths, two mounds: he was burning her, very slowly.

Where are you going? she thought she heard him ask. She thought she said *home* but she couldn't be certain. She didn't know where she was going anymore. She wanted someone to take her far away from herself.

Something in her bowels was beginning to tighten. She was wet between her legs. She realized she wanted him to touch her down there, to stroke away the fear.

Where do you think you're going? she thought she heard him ask. She was not thinking. She had no power to think: he had taken the power from her. He had taken her into his consciousness and changed her. She no longer existed. She was no longer the same person.

But she could feel him touching her. Stroking her face, her neck, her chest. He was touching her face with his cold, meaty hands. Pawing her breasts, pinching her nipples. He had a huge erection, he was pressing it into her.

He knew she wanted him. He knew she didn't.

Lie down, he told her, and she did. Spruce needles prickled the skin on her back; she squirmed as he slid his hand down into her pants.

He pulled off her trousers and made her spread her legs. He knelt down between them and struck another match.

He held the match a few inches from the lips of her vagina. *Let's see it*, he said. *Show me.*

She was swollen, she could feel, as she parted her lips for him. He'd see that she was excited, he'd be able to see the moisture.

Her temperature was rising, the moisture turning to steam. *The finger has to fit properly, has to be tight enough but not too tight . . .*

He put his finger inside her, slowly, as far up as it would go. Her muscles tensed and relaxed as she took hold of it, drawing it in like a sea anemone. She was opening and feeding, full of secret juices. The finger lolled, unmoving, between the lips of her vulva.

Her head was aching. She wanted something deeper, something she wasn't getting. She wanted the finger to satisfy, to fill the emptiness. She wanted two fingers, a whole hand. Anything to stop the dead feeling.

No pain, no. She didn't want that. Why was he hurting her? She didn't want his love.

He was withdrawing his finger, taking it out slowly, as if it were something he had just found, half-alive, inside her. Something the sea anemone had spit out in disgust. Something too devious to be consumed and digested.

He had a ring on his finger, a wolf running in circles until he was swallowed by darkness, circles of darkness that moved towards her then moved away again.

Christian's ring. Rasputin held it up to his face, and the silver lit his eyes.

26

For the remainder of the week Matty stayed locked in the dormitory. She slept most of the time, without dreaming. She felt obliterated; she perceived everything around her as shadows. Even Hot Stuff when he came to her door with food – she never ate anything for fear of being poisoned – was not real to her. He looked like a visitor from an alien planet, with pale yellow eyes and mushroom-coloured skin.

She hardly cared whether it was day or night. She didn't mind the rats anymore; they kept her company. They wouldn't touch her food either, and by the third day they'd learned enough not even to bother sniffing at it.

On the evening of the fifth day Hot Stuff came to fetch her. Reptile was opening the kiln, he said, and they wanted her to be there. She felt little sensation as he led her into the clean air. Light and dark had become almost the same thing. When her eyes were open they might as well have been closed; she could no longer tell the difference.

Black Sam, Crow Bait, and General Electric had gathered in the clearing; Crow Bait's pit had exploded and there was nothing left but a hole in the ground. The three looked at Matty as if she were a haunch of venison being brought home from a hunt. Even the rats had not looked at her so inhumanly.

She sat down next to the kiln; Hot Stuff brought her a cup of tea. She realized that she must have grown thinner, like the kiln itself which had shrunk during the process of burning. The kiln had been reduced to the size of a large beehive. She looked like a skeleton.

Reptile removed the outer covering of the kiln, exposing the charred turf. He smoothed the surface, scraping off the loose dust, then added a layer of fresh damp earth to make sure the kiln was air-tight again. He sprinkled the mound with water, explaining that it might catch fire. He spoke to Matty as if nothing had gone wrong, as if nothing had happened since the last time she'd sat there listening to him talk.

On the sheltered side he raked the inner layer away. With a long-pronged fork he drew the charcoal out of the pit, working as quickly as possible to prevent the kiln from flaming.

Hot Stuff spread the charcoal on the ground and sprinkled it with more water. Crow Bait suggested they save some of the coals so they would have a fire going when it came time to cook dinner.

"We'll have that stuff I pickled a few weeks ago," said the General. "I've been saving it for, you know, a special occasion."

They looked at Matty, the three of them with their little pig-eyes. She didn't care what happened to her now, she was beyond being hurt by them.

Black Sam frowned. "Someone should tell Rasputin to get his ass down here. He's the only one who can cook that shit."

"Look, man, who corned it?" said Crow Bait. "It would have gotten bad without the General knowing what to do. You know what I mean, like it would have gone rotten. That's a real bummer, man, I mean like that's a pretty heavy number."

"The General don't know how to *cook*, man," said Black Sam, shaking his head in disgust. "So what you intend on doing with that shit, eh boy? You gonna cook it yourself?"

"We'll get *her* to cook it," said the General, nodding at Matty. The three looked at her and grinned, conspiratorially. "She's got nothing better to do, anyway," he continued, "so she can go up there and get it, too. It'll be like a kind of adventure, you know? Seems to me there's been no *excitement* around here lately."

Hot Stuff went on sorting the charcoal. He and Reptile seemed oblivious to the other men. Matty experienced everything from a distance: Hot Stuff picking the half-charred bits of charcoal from the heap and setting them aside to fill the chimney of the next kiln had no more reality than the three little pig-men bickering over their dinner.

Reptile loaded the good charcoal into sacks and Hot Stuff put the sacks in a wheelbarrow. He motioned Matty to follow him.

They walked back to camp, to the shed where the charcoal was stored. The shed was adjacent to hers, her bunkhouse, and the door, normally padlocked, had been left wide open.

Hot Stuff told her to help unload the charcoal and they spread it out on the floor inside. It should have been left by the pit to cool for longer, he told her, but he didn't trust the others. Last time they'd scattered it about, trying to make a fire, and half the yield had been ruined. Reptile, as usual, had been too busy thinking; he hardly ever noticed what other people were doing.

"Meat's in the back," said Hot Stuff. "You can use the wheelbarrow if you need it. They'll want three or four good pieces, at least. There are some garbage bags to wrap it in."

She was prepared for anything. A two-headed pig foetus, pickled in a jar, with thorns stuck through its testicles and yellow ribbons tied to its tail, or Siamese twins, fused together at the belly and sharing a common navel, floating face-up in a vat full of brine: nothing would surprise her.

"I'll send Rasputin," Hot Stuff added. "You won't be able to cook that stuff yourself."

"Rasputin." She said his name aloud – it was the first word

she'd spoken since leaving the dormitory – not in fear but as an affirmation. She was still alive, still had some will left, in spite of his attempts to defeat her. She'd willed herself into passivity where nothing, not even the most gruesome discovery, could hurt her.

She helped Hot Stuff unload the last of the charcoal and sat down to rest until he'd gone. He left the door open and the shed was filled with sun. Lying along the eastern wall was a row of wooden trunks.

They were shaped like small coffins and padlocked. She tried to imagine the contents – passports, property deeds, photographs, identification papers, jewellery, cheque books, rolls of cash, charred remains of her deceased predecessors. The thought didn't upset her; she had willed herself not to feel anything. She tested herself, imagining the worst possibilities, and felt nothing.

Against the back wall there were eight tubs. She lifted off their covers; six contained meat and the other two, fat and bones. She reached down into a meat tub; something brushed her hand. It felt cold and slippery. She dropped it again immediately.

Hot Stuff had said there were plastic garbage bags. She searched the room until she discovered them, lying under a sack stained with blood and charcoal. There was a book inside the sack – some kind of ledger. She sat down on one of the chests, turning the pages, slowly.

The name, date, size, and description of every carcass that had ever been pickled was recorded in the book. Men, women, and babies were listed under the category of "Rare Meat" while animals fell under "Other." She took the piece of paper from her pocket, the one she'd found on the floor of her dormitory, and compared it to the ledger. The page had obviously been torn from the same book, and the unfinished poem had been entered in the same handwriting:

R's the butcher, S likes rare meat,
General Electric corns the beef.

It was Hot Stuff's writing, she recognized it. She'd seen him making notes while the kiln was burning.

She put the ledger down. She took a garbage bag and filled it with the meat. Afterwards, when she'd replaced the lids, firmly, on each of the vats, she loaded the bag onto the wheelbarrow.

Her own name had been entered in the ledger, right beneath Christian and Dan's. Her entry, unlike theirs, was not dated, and they'd got her physical description wrong. It said her eyes were grey – she remembered them as being blue. She found herself wondering if their colour might have changed. It was the only thought she had as she pushed the wheelbarrow back over the rough ground.

"So you won't eat?" said Rasputin, thrusting his half-devoured meat in Matty's direction. "When you're starving you'll change your mind. You won't always be so fussy."

Rasputin had forced her, at knife-point, to sit with them while they ate. He'd cooked her some of the meat, but she had refused it.

Reptile was starting another kiln in the hole where Crow Bait's had exploded. It was an odd place to build, Matty thought, and he had not prepared the ground carefully.

"It's a test pit," said Hot Stuff, taking her by the arm. "An experiment. You'll help us."

The first billets formed a large triangle. Hot Stuff told Matty to stand in the middle of the triangle as they wanted to check the chimney for width.

It was just wide enough for her body. Reptile piled the branches up as high as her waist, long spindly branches of a freshly fallen spruce, building a triangular chimney around her. She was starting to sweat. Blackflies crawled in under her collar; blood and sweat trickled down the back of her neck.

Hot Stuff told her to climb out and they continued building until the chimney was six feet high. There was no doubt in her mind, now, that the kiln was intended for her.

The thought of her imminent death didn't bother her. Her mind had already made the transition. She had died anyway when she'd stopped having feelings. It was her body that was the problem. It kept on living.

By midnight the kiln was nearly completed. Reptile and Hot Stuff were starting on the cover while the rest of the men went on eating and drinking. Crow Bait had swallowed a second tab of acid, hoping it would help him "get his head together."

"Ever eaten eyes?" said Rasputin, looking at the General. "They say that's the best part, especially if you get them young. Before they've had a chance to look around, you know?"

The General said there was a section on eye-gouging in his U.S. Fighting Manual. "You put one thumb on the inside of the eye-socket and another one on the nose. Then you flick the eyeball out towards the edge of the cheek. I seen it done. There was pictures."

"I hope there's no more war, man," said Crow Bait.

"Some people like the heart," said Rasputin. "You dry it, grind it up and mix it with rum. How you doing there, C.B.? Pass the bottle over this-away."

"Where's Hot Stuff, that bum?" said the General. "We need some more of this. Hey, Sam! Cat got your tongue? Ever eaten a heart? Eh, you dumb nigger!"

Sam nodded, staring wide-eyed into the fire.

"Like all the lights are on," said Crow Bait, looking at him, "but nobody's home."

"He's pissed," said the General.

Rasputin took the lid off his stew pot. He fished out a large chunk of meat and put it on the General's plate.

"Brains," he said. "Peking man ate brains and bone marrow."

"Filthy chinks," said the General. He pushed his plate into Matty's lap. "Brains," he said. "You need some."

Pickled brain, a three-pound human sponge made of grey cells and silent areas. She removed the dish from her lap and placed it on the ground beside her.

"What's wrong with you?" asked Crow Bait, unzipping and pissing on the fire. "I mean like why aren't you eating anything? Don't you eat meat, or what? I mean like, aren't you going to try it? It's really far-out."

"Shut your mouth," snapped the General. "You're talking to a *lady.*"

"What's wrong with asking her if she doesn't eat meat?" said Crow Bait. "Like I don't see what's wrong with asking her that, man. I mean like, really." He let go of his penis and left it hanging out, like a little cocktail sausage.

"Put that thing away," said the General, punching him and knocking him backwards. "You don't leave it out in front of a lady, you dumb cunt. Where's your respect?"

He turned his back on Crow Bait and moved closer to Rasputin. "There was this story I read somewhere," he said, "about these guys who used to piss on charcoal–just like Crow Bait does. And what happened was their dinks dropped off. All of them. Every goddamn one!" He grabbed his genitals and fell off the log, howling.

"You asshole," Rasputin laughed, catching hold of the bottle as the log began to tip. "You got the whole story backasswards. They don't piss, they shit. They squat over these pits. I mean that's how they keep warm. It's too fuckin' cold to go outside to shit. For fuck's sake get your facts right."

"I'd still like to know what I did wrong," whined Crow Bait. "All I said was 'don't you eat meat' and now everybody's acting hostile."

"Forget it," said the General, slapping him on the back. "I'm sorry, okay? Just forget about it."

He rolled another joint and passed it along to Crow Bait. Black Sam had fallen asleep where he was sitting, with bits of meat and gravy all down the front of his clothes.

"Why should he forget it?" said Rasputin, suddenly.

"When you come to think about it, he's got every right to know." He turned to Matty, grinning. "Well, do you or don't you. Do vegetarians give blow-jobs or don't they?"

But Matty wasn't there. She'd been backing away from the fire, gradually, and nobody had noticed. When she saw Rasputin turn to her she crouched down in the shadows, hoping he wouldn't see her. Rasputin gave a shout and lunged. He grabbed her by the ankle, twisted it, and sent her sprawling.

"The man wants to know," he said, dragging her back to the fire, "and I say you owe him an answer. What do you think, boys? Does she or doesn't she?"

Crow Bait handed the General the half-empty bottle, giggling stupidly. "I mean like you're the butcher–you should know," he said to Rasputin. "I mean you should know for sure, man. Know what I mean?"

"Got you, C.B.," said Rasputin. He put his arm around Matty's neck and forced her head back, roughly. "Hey, General! Hand me the bottle! Can't you see–the lady needs a drink!" His fingers tightened around her throat. "Open up," he said, digging into her neck. "If you know what's good for you, you'll do what you're told."

She pinched her lips and clenched her teeth. The whisky was poisonous. She didn't want to drink.

He struck her across the mouth, driving her front teeth deep into her quivering lower lip.

"If you want to keep your teeth, drink it," he whispered, ramming the bottle into the back of her throat. The whisky burned; it was drowning her. Whisky and blood poured out of her nose. If she didn't gulp it down she knew she would suffocate.

He tilted the bottle back until it was empty. Then he let her go. She spat. She ran her tongue over her teeth. Her teeth were chipped and her mouth was full of bone-grit.

The General snatched the bottle from Rasputin's hands.

"She killed it, the bitch!" he cried. "She drank *all* of it!"

She took a deep breath and spat again. Her teeth were going to drop out. She needed a dentist.

She was going to be sick. She needed a doctor. The bottle was in her mouth again and they had forced her on her back. Maybe they were going to choke her, finish her off quickly. She tried to struggle but her attempts were useless.

"Lie still and you won't get hurt," Rasputin ordered. "C.B., get the rope. General, you hold her."

Rasputin pulled Matty to her feet and they dragged her to the abandoned pit. The General held her down while Rasputin tied her, spreadeagled, to the burnt mound.

The kiln was still warm. What if it suddenly started to catch? Where was Reptile to regulate the burning?

Rasputin stuck the bottle back in her mouth. She tried to spit it out; it was useless.

"Suck, baby, suck," said the General. "*Blow* is only the word they use." He punched Crow Bait again, who crumpled, like a punching bag without stuffing. The General collapsed beside him, laughing. He beat the air with his fists, crying "*suck, suck*" to Matty who had the bottle.

Glass and grit in her mouth. Broken teeth and whisky.

"Have a good taste," said Rasputin, with his knee in her stomach. "You won't get anything else to drink."

She let her mouth relax; she stopped resisting.

"Suck it," said Rasputin, "in and out. You're feeling sick now, aren't you? That'll teach you to drink all of Hot Stuff's whisky. You won't be so greedy again, will you? *Will you.*"

He slapped her again, backhanded, across the face. He grabbed a handful of hair and pulled it, tearing it out by the roots. She screamed; she could hardly feel anything but the blood on the ground was proof. It was her blood; she had been wounded. Still she heard the scream coming from somebody else's body.

Kill cancer, said Crow Bait. Was she cancer?

Kill the Jews, said the General. Was she a Jew?

"Don't let go of that bottle," Rasputin said to her. "I want you to hold that bottle in your mouth."

Ban the bomb, said Crow Bait.

Kill for peace, said the General.

She couldn't see anything. Something–the whisky–had blinded her.

She didn't want this. Anything would have been preferable. The rats, the darkness, death, the locked dormitory. Life there, in comparison, had been utter bliss.

Bliss piss.

She understood, finally, what was happening. The glass, the blood, the poison, their words: suddenly everything had become real to her. The ropes cut into her flesh, into her alive, warm, sensitive flesh. Why did they want her to feel so much when she'd already surrendered and there was nothing left to kill.

There was something. There was her body. Her spirit was very willing to give up everything but her body was not weak, and would not die.

The bottle was heavy. "Hold it in your mouth. Careful," said Rasputin. "Don't bite it. I don't want you to hurt my bottle. I don't want any marks on it. It's an old, old friend of mine, see? So don't drop it!"

It was too heavy to hold. She *would* drop it, let it smash at his feet. That would show him. He could go ahead and kill her.

Bottle bitten bliss piss.

"That's it. Hold it between your lips. If you suck hard enough you won't drop it."

The bottle was getting lighter. Her lips were going numb. With her head weighted and bowed she saw him draw the cleaver from his jacket. She heard the sound of steel against stone, of rough against smooth, sharp against dull, day against night. Her flesh, his knife. His laugh, her life.

"Don't drop it," he repeated. He bent down, cleaver between his teeth, and began to untie her bootlaces.

That was it. He was going to chop off her feet. Cut them off at the ankles so she could never get away.

She heard the sound of fabric being cut. He was slicing up the inside of her trousers, from her ankle to her crotch, and down the other side again, tearing and cutting. He nicked her thigh leaving a bright seam of blood.

On the outside of her legs he cut from the waist down leaving her trousers in shreds. Strips of heavy woollen fabric dangled from her middle like gauze bandages. Rasputin slipped an oily finger between her legs, and smiled smugly. Fear had made her wet. He knew he had that power.

He slit from the wrists to the armpits of her sweater and down the sides of her body. He cut along the outside of her sweater, up the arms, to the neck. He sliced holes for breasts and caressed her nipples with the dull edge of the knife. Crow Bait and the General began fondling one another.

Her sweater clung to her like the last leaves of a tree in winter. She felt like a scarecrow, crucified in a field of vultures. Like the scarecrow on the altar after her Pregnancy Wishes Ritual. Tattered and broken in her own image.

"First you must take off all your clothes," she could hear Celandine saying. It was Arrack's formula and only to be used in an emergency. *"Then you must visualize an imaginary door. You must stand in front of this door, with your arms outstretched like a cross, and say to yourself:* In the midst of life we are in death. *Say these words three times, and the third time mentally impress the words on the door. If the spell has worked the door will spring open. Then you can pass through it and on the other side you'll be invisible."*

Matty closed her eyes, trying to imagine a door. There was no way out, there was nothing.

"Blow-jobs!" shouted Crow Bait, taking his hand out of the General's pocket.

"Blow-jobs!" shouted the General. He kicked Black Sam who fell over into the fire. Matty could smell his hair burning. Nobody bothered to move him.

Rasputin looked at his men. He looked at Matty. He put his

hands between her legs and squeezed her lips together. She flinched. He pinched harder.

Then he removed the bottle from her mouth and untied her body from the kiln. She slumped onto the ground. Rasputin wanted to know how much of the bottle she could take inside her. She didn't respond until he twisted her arm and threatened to cut off her ears and her fingers.

"Now you can fuck the bottle," he said. "You're wet enough. We all know you want it. You heard the boys. They want blow-jobs. Give them a show. Something to liven things up. They've been out in the bush too long. Give them a good time. They're ready."

He closed her hand around the bottle and spread her legs. "Come on. Put it in. Push it up. Push harder."

The bottle slipped easily between the lips of her vulva. It made a small sucking sound. Crow Bait wanted to play Spin the Bottle; the General bragged that he had the world's fattest cock, fatter even than the bottle Crow Bait wanted to play with. Matty couldn't think: she just wanted to die. As long as she lived they would go on hurting her.

The General was getting bored. "What are we waiting for?" he argued. "I mean, this is all very romantic, but what about *us*? Why should *she* be having all the fun? Come on, Rasputin. Let me at her!"

"Come on, Rasputin! I mean like, let me at her," Crow Bait parroted.

Rasputin nodded. "Okay. The General goes first and then it's your turn, C.B. Sam isn't into it. Are you, Sammy?"

"He's on fire," said the General. "I thought I could smell someone burning."

Rasputin kicked him out of the fire and smothered the flames with his jacket. The General grabbed the bottle away from Matty and threw it at Black Sam's head. The bottle bounced, hit a rock, and shattered.

"Like he's heavily into sleep," said Crow Bait.

The General shook his head. "He got fried," he said.

"Lucky for him he was already that colour."

Rasputin shook Matty. She was like a rag-doll lying curled up with the twisted ankle tucked under her.

"Sit up," he said. "Look what you've done to Sam. What have you got to say about that? If it hadn't been for you we would have saved him."

All the words were gone. All the warmth was gone and all the reason. There was nothing left inside her but pain. Nothing but pain and sadness.

She wanted to speak but the words had left her. She stared at Rasputin but there was nothing to see. She shivered; they thought it was all one big joke. Of course she was joking. She began to laugh with them.

The General struck her. She fell to the ground, laughing. She would let them take her, she would die laughing. She would go to her grave laughing. She would laugh her way into the afterlife.

The General pulled her back onto her knees. "Give me a blow-job, bitch! Suck it, use your tongue!"

She stared at him but she couldn't see anything. What was she supposed to suck? What tongue?

"Fish it out with your mouth. Don't use your hands. Hurry up! *Do* it!"

Her mouth laughing. Her tongue laughing. She touched his cold zipper with all its cold, hard laughter. Her hands laughing. Her chipped teeth laughing as they pulled the zipper down.

There was no penis inside his pants, no laughter. The General was limp; there was no battle. There was no laughter anywhere. Only defeat.

Matty smiled. She had learned how to laugh without anybody hearing her. She laughed at the emptiness, laughed about the laughter. She laughed at the General's battering ram which had shrivelled into the size of a pink eraser.

She took the whole of it in her mouth. She heard more laughter. He hadn't been circumcized and his foreskin was full of laughter. She tried to make him hard but the laughter grew stronger.

The General pulled out, shaking. The inside of her mouth, he said, was like sandpaper.

Crow Bait stepped forward, nervously. He had an exceptionally small erection and it obviously embarrassed him. Matty wet her hand and touched him. Crow Bait came in her hair.

The laughter swallowed her. She looked at Black Sam but he was still unconscious. The General said that Sam wasn't missing anything anyway, that Crow Bait was perverted and could get it up for a dog.

The laughter began to hurt. She was laughing and crying at the same time and it all hurt.

Rasputin became a ringing in her ears. Crow Bait was an ache, the General a cold light burning behind her eyes. The darkness became a sea; she heard the cold waves breaking. It was a comforting sound. Rasputin was water and she was drowning in him.

They dragged her body further into the trees. Rasputin took her head in his left hand, twisting it upward. He held the knife in his right hand. Light flashed on the blade, and Matty flinched.

It was the knife that made her flinch, not the gurgle that rose from deep within her body, nor the gaping wound she could picture at her neck. It was the clean stroke of the knife: she waited for it. She relived her life, over and over, in slow motion.

It didn't matter. Nothing mattered.

Matty was on a roller coaster high above the sea. Down below she could see Christian, wearing his old green jacket, and Dan, standing beside him, his face a mask of death.

Her mother was there, too, laughing because Matty was coming to join them. The roller coaster was falling and the sea was full of fins.

Christian couldn't save her; he had no head. Dan was

swimming out to sea but the current was stronger and was pulling him apart. The fins formed a circle around him, slowly closing in, a whirlpool of fins that finally sucked him under.

"As waves come with water and flames with fire, the universe waves with us," said her mother. She was waving a white handkerchief, waving out and over the blue horizon.